WHAT THE EYES SEE

CAN YOUR EYES ALWAYS SEE THE TRUTH ?

NITYA RAVI

Invincible Publishers

First Printing: 2019

ISBN: 978-93-89600-12-4

Invincible Publishers

Registered Address: 201A, SAS Tower, Sector 38, Gurgaon - 122003

This is for you Dad and Mom...
For being patient with me always.

Table of Contents

Author's note

For many years, I had this dream of publishing my book, which never materialized mostly due to my downright laziness and procrastination. There, I have said it on a public platform.

This book and the short stories in it, is a leap of faith I have taken on my writing and in the hope of entertaining all of you.

If you ask me what genre would these stories fall into, my answer would be 'a big shrug'. You can call it dark, suspense, dare I say horror or to put it simple- just some stories for time pass. As long as you enjoy reading them, that's all the happiness I want.

Maybe by the end of this book you might feel that I have given some sort of prominence, at least in a subtle way into the grey areas of human behavior. I am a person who believes that all of us have that grey area in our character and for me what scares me more than ghosts, spirits or the likes is the darkness of the human mind especially with the ones who think it's alright to hurt someone.

I enjoyed writing these stories and really hope you love them too.

Much love

Nitya Ravi.

If you loved my work, please do review me on Amazon.com. You can also follow me on instagram on - ***authornityaravi***, on facebook at - ***@authornityaravi*** or even email me your feedback at ravi.nitya@gmail.com. I would love to hear from you.

What the eyes see and the ears hear, the mind believes.

- Harry Houdini (Illusionist and stunt performer)

SIRA

"By far the greatest danger of Artificial Intelligence is that people conclude too early that they understand it."

- Eliezer Yudkowsky

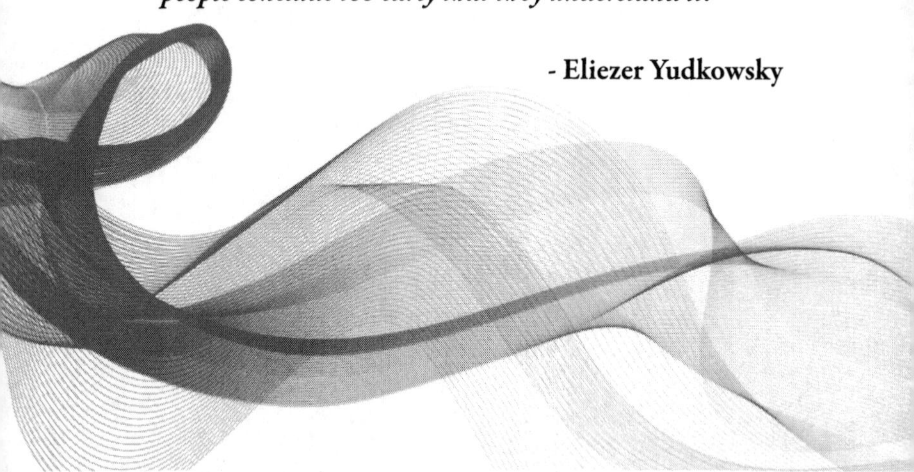

1

I remember there was a time when humans used to do most of the things in life. There was more of human intelligence and less of artificial intelligence.

Today the ratio has changed.

They are everywhere now. Factories, roads, shops, schools, banks–you name it and they were there–these 'things'.

We also learned ways to extend our life. Currently, I am 65 years old but I function and even almost look like a 40 year old.

It was considered a revolution in genetic engineering, which helped alter the damaged cells in our body. All it took was a shot–a 'miracle shot', like how it was known to the layman–a very expensive shot administered directly into your blood. A week or two of feeling utterly sick followed by feeling strong and youthful after that. Life gets extended by at least 10 years. This shot was mostly used to combat cancer cells in ailing patients.

Is that good? I am sure it's not.

We were messing with nature!

My thoughts and my writing were interrupted by SIRA. She is my new help.

'Time for your chai, Sir.' She smiled at me.

'SIRA, please leave it at the table. You know very well I do not like to be disturbed while am working.'

'I am sorry, Sir. I was lost in my thoughts...please excuse me.' She hesitated and left the room in a hurry.

Thoughts my foot...what thoughts? You can never be a human, SIRA.

I got up and looked out of the window. The day was bright and beautiful though I felt a bit tired. I walked towards the full-length mirror on the side of my bedroom and looked at myself. People still call me handsome though I don't feel the same anymore. My hair and my beard were white though my body looked otherwise. If only the damn robot had not disturbed me, I could have finished this piece today. SIRA had disturbed my train of thoughts.

I had bought SIRA 2 years ago when cancer had got the better of me. That it was eating into my body for a year was something that I had never realized. When the doctors told me that I had to undergo chemo, I wasn't ready for that either. Then they asked me if I wanted to take the 'miracle shot'.

I told them I wasn't rich enough for the same.

My wife Maya was taken away by cancer too but that was a long time ago. 10 years to be precise. The 'miracle shot' was in the first stages of development then and so she did not have that option available.

After Maya's death and the children moving out for their jobs and studies, I was all alone. I took care of everything myself. I was used to staying alone and caring for myself and totally abhorred the idea of getting a total stranger into my house or in this case, a total strange THING into my house.

There were no more human helps available for home and thus the only option were these things with circuits and softwares in place of a proper human brain; so suffer I did in silence with my growing cancer until my daughter Shradda stepped in and offered to buy SIRA for me. My firstborn Shradda loved me a lot. I was too proud to go and stay with her or my son Amit. This ailing old man did not want to be a burden on them and so she pleaded and begged me to at least keep help at home until finally, I relented but I told her I would buy SIRA myself. Thus came SIRA to my home.

SIRA was so strong. I can't believe I called her a SHE. However, she looked like a SHE, she had the voice of a SHE and that also of a kind-hearted SHE but she was strong enough to take on any man.

She came with a catalog of many Indian dishes (North, South, East and West) and would easily whip up any dish I asked for and that too tasty ones. She cleaned my house, took care of my medications, and even served me chai or coffee on time but I still couldn't bring myself to warm to her presence in my home. For some reason, I did not trust these machines and hence I found it extremely difficult to trust her either.

The first time I had a vague idea of how strong she was, was when she swung a charging German shepherd away from me and whisked it onto the road as if it was a fly. It had smashed onto the wall and died. The dog was later found to be rabid. The incident shook me up and rather than making me feel safe, it made me feel unsafe. I just kept thinking that if required, she can even pick ME up from the floor, swing me if she wants to or maybe smash me on the wall.

Later one day, pick me she did when I fainted from the sheer agony of the pain that was growing in my body and eating me up. I woke up to her looking at me, tenderness in her eyes.

'I called your kids. They are on their way to see you'

'Who asked you to?' I scolded her.

SIRA did not reply to this. She looked upset...or did she? Can these things feel anything at all?

I drifted back to sleep to awaken later to my son and daughter beside me along with Dr. Rajan, our family doctor. After making sure I was ok, he asked me to come and visit him in the clinic the next day and left.

'When we lost mom, we couldn't do anything papa. At least allow us to help YOU.' My daughter almost pleaded with me.

'Shradda...I cannot keep giving in to your demands because I love you,' and I meant that.

How can I tell her that I am kind of fed up of living this lonely life? I had started having dreams of my wife, my best friend, my parents, even my sister (who died tragically in a car crash)–everyone from my generation and before who died.

From the corner of my eye, I saw SIRA looking at us with something akin to deep concern in her eyes.

I wanted to ask her to leave the room and I guess she understood. She straightened up suddenly and mechanically, giving out the fact she was a machine after all and walked out of the room leaving us alone.

My son who was silent all this while looked at me, 'It's your birthday this coming May.'

'Yes, but I don't think I will be alive until then.' I said grimly.

'But PAPA! You are even refusing chemo!' He was very upset.

'Papa, I can afford this treatment. Please allow me to get it for you as a gift on your birthday. We want you to be with us for some more time.' Amit was pleading now. He knows very well about my ego (that I don't like to depend on my children for money) and I know very well that he can afford this for me if I would just say a yes. He was one of the leading movie stars of the country. That he would get into the acting field and is on his way to being one of the most successful actors in the country is something I haven't still digested. Growing up, he was just like any other child – never felt there was a bone of talent in that boy. But he blindsided all of us.

He did not even inform us that he was trying his luck in acting until he signed his very first movie. It wasn't anything major. It was a small-time movie. But we supported him and slowly he grew. I watched one of his movies and was proud to see him up on that screen owning the space.

'You know that I can't and don't want to.' I answered Amit

At this, my daughter looking very solemn asked Amit to leave the room. She wanted to talk to me in private.

Amit looked at her and nodded his head. He stepped out of the room but left the door slightly ajar.

'Papa...' Shradda started to say something and ended up crying instead.

Being her father, it's always been difficult for me to watch her cry. It affected me like nothing ever. It's been the same since she was a child. There were many times when Maya used to scold me when she saw me giving into Shradda's whims whenever she cried.

'That girl will take you for a ride. Please don't spoil her,' she used to scold me.

But no, my child was not spoilt. She grew up to be a fine young lady – into the most understanding and caring person I know. People loved her. She today owns one of the finest labels in the fashion industry and is busy with her work and family. She married a man she met at the University and together they have two beautiful girls aged 5 and 3 who are my world.

She did not reply at first to my concern over her crying. I guess she was stressed about the fact that I won't be around for too long but then I had made up my mind.

'Ram is not like before. He is very abusive nowadays.' Shradda's words caught me off guard.

'What do you mean?' I tried to get up. The pain bolted up to my stomach.

'Calls me names...the other day, he almost hit me. I think...he is seeing someone else'.

A different type of pain got hold of me now. It was concentrated in my heart. I felt rage built up in me. No one dares to raise a hand on my children.

But Ram? How can he do this?

When Shradda had first announced to me about the guy she was planning to marry, I knew that her choice would not be wrong. After all, she was someone who had her head on her shoulders, aware of what's going on around her and capable of living life on her terms.

When I first met Ram, I wasn't disappointed either. He was a gentleman and there was pure love radiating from his eyes whenever he was with her. I knew he would take good care of her and he did keep up that thought of mine—until today.

'How long is he been like this?'

'Quite some time. I really don't like the girls seeing or hearing this. It distresses me a lot.' She said looking lost and started sobbing again.

'Have you tried talking to him?' I managed to ask despite the pain.

She was silent for sometime before she continued, 'If I talk to him Papa, I must be sure that am ready to leave him in case he...in case he doesn't care to change.'

I did not say anything to that. I did not know what to tell her.

'Papa, I want you to be around. There are days I wish Maa was still alive. But that isn't so and now I have only you. Being a mother and raising two girls... It's so difficult to always be strong in front of them ...I think inside me a small girl still resides who wish to run to her parents whenever she feels things are getting too much for her. There are nights I have stayed awake trying not to cry unable to bear the burden of this...Mom not being around, raising the girls, Ram's behavior and us drifting apart and knowing that soon even you would leave us...' She looked at me with tears brimming in her eyes.

'I wouldn't have even mentioned all this right now but when Science is ready to help us be with our dear ones for a longer period and especially if we can afford it, I want you to at least try it out. I want you to be with us, Papa. We need you. I need you. '

She was crying again.

I hugged her and allowed her to cry, my heart very heavy. I did not know what to say that would make her feel better. But I surely knew what I had to do that would make her feel better. My heart was torn into two, unable to decide.

'We will get this resolved Shradda... don't worry...I am there for you and I will be there for you. I am not leaving you. I know I have been...selfish.'

Outside I felt a movement and called out to check who it was but there was no response.

Shradda managed to smile now. 'Looks like Amit wants to hear what we are discussing just like old times, remember when he used to sneak up on us discussing about things?'

I nodded, though unconvinced that it was Amit.

Amit later denied the same and I believed him. I am sure I know who it was and that gave me an uneasy feeling.

2

Shradda thus managed to change my mind and I got the miracle shot. A few days of utter sickness followed where I vomited and slept a lot. Dr. Rajan visited me morning, afternoon and evening to ensure I was ok. I told him I wasn't going to admit myself in the hospital, which was what people usually did when the shot was administered. So I was put in the delicate care of SIRA, who kept feeding me lots of water and other liquids to make up for the water I lost from my body. She took me to bath, changed my bedclothes, my clothes and fed me mostly liquid food strictly and on time.

At times I would get angry at her for even trying to give me food. I would yell at her and she would leave the food at the table and be gone. But she would be back soon after to check and to irritate me again about the same. I was too weak to protest any further or to be stubborn.

Sometimes to keep her away I would eat whatever she brought me. She would smile tenderly (I despised that smile) whenever she saw that I have eaten and take the plates away humming some old Hindi tune.

After the puking spree, I had two days of very high fever, which was followed by two days of extreme pain spread over my entire body. I was warned of all these side effects which they said will only last for a few days but when it hit me, I wasn't ready for it and even wondered if I have made a big mistake. SIRA took care of me through it all, keeping my temperature in check and making me take my medications on time.

A week later, I got up to a morning of feeling extremely healthy and wonderful. It was as if I had regained all my lost energy.

I got up from my bed to look into the mirror in my bedroom. What I saw there gave me a rather pleasant surprise.

My face, which used to be tired and haggard, looked like someone had injected it with the youth serum. It looked almost wrinkle-free and fresh – shining with health. I couldn't believe it! I touched the face on the mirror before bringing my hand back to my face to touch my skin

What if when I touch, it ends up being just a dream?

But no, it was no dream. It was me indeed. I smiled. Grinned rather. A sort of happiness burst out of me.

The pain and fever were gone and so was the nausea and vomiting.

I came out of my room to find SIRA putting my tea on the table. 'I heard you wake up sir. Here is your tea,' She said smiling

'How do I look SIRA?' I asked her.

'You look amazing Sir! Wow, what a change!' the expressions they have managed to stitch on her face amaze me.

I smiled back at her before proceeding to call my kids. For a moment then I thanked Science and all the advances it has made because of which I could feel this way. I was sure my cancer had gone for a toss. I could feel it. I could feel it missing from my body. It was as if the last one-week was a process of eliminating the goddamn cancer out of my body. Little did I know that I would regret it later ...very...very much.

3

It's been a year now since I cheated cancer with the miracle shot.

Shradda and Ram decided to part ways. He was indeed cheating on her with another woman and he confessed the same to her. He was not in love with the woman he was cheating with but it seems he had fallen out of love with Shradda too and wanted time to figure out things.

Shradda opted for divorce. I know her heart was heavy when she did it because she loves that good-for-nothing loser like anything but she was a brave girl. She loved herself and her children more and she knew the girls couldn't grow up in an unhealthy environment.

I never talked to him. I knew that if I did, I might want to break his hands for touching my daughter.

As for me, I decided to write a book. I always wanted to write and there have been times while I was working as one of the top strategists of an international IT vendor, that I wished to write but time was never on my side and my passion was mostly directed towards my work. Writing was my next passion. Whenever I got the time, I wrote poems, short stories and the likes, and many a times Maya had asked me to write a full-fledged novel since she felt that I was an ace writer. Maya was always encouraging and motivating. However she knew this would need a cut from our time together, she would still keep pushing me to go ahead with my dream. I still couldn't do it while she was alive. I wanted to do it now.

Now that I was not working anymore and had enough money to keep me thriving and living in comfort and also some real estate I was renting out, I had time in my hands to do what I always wanted to do. The miracle shot just gave me the energy to do all the things I aspired for.

Amit was very amused at my idea to write. The fact that he was in his 30s and still unmarried was not because of a dearth of women who loved him, he just decided to be unmarried.

'It's a lot of complication. I don't want to be bound to anyone. It's a different type of responsibility that I do not want to take.'

We keep telling him that he hasn't met the right woman yet and once he does, all this *gyaan* of his will go down the drain. But he sticks to what he thinks is right. Good for him; as long as he is happy. I don't interfere too much in anyone's life, unless asked to.

Right now he was out of the country on his much-needed break after wrapping up shoot for his latest movie.

'You want to write? Like really?' I heard him laughing.

'Cut it out. What is there to laugh so much about?' I chided. He was on a video call from Italy where he was for his vacation. His infectious smile that the country has come to love lightened up my screen.

'Nothing Pa...am so happy to see you like this. Do anything you want – write, act, sing, jump, skydive, bungee jump, even fall in love!'

'No am not up for that. My heart is dried up.' I said laughing.

We spoke for some more time about the climate in Italy and the political situation in India, his new movie coming up and then called it a day. It was time for my evening tea.

I turned to see SIRA already in the room. The cup of tea and a plate of biscuits were on my table.

Every morning and afternoon SIRA would come with my medications and my tea. I am to take these till the day I die. It is to control some after-effects of the miracle shot.

'How long you been here?' I asked her, a bit taken aback. It was like she tiptoed into the room.

'Oh I just came.' she said nonchalantly.

'SIRA... next time I am on a video call, I want you to knock the door hard before you enter. Am I clear?'

She nodded at that and smiled. I did not like that smile.

'What is it? Why that smile?' I asked.

'Oh, nothing Sir. I like the way you are with your son. You are like buddies.'

I did not react to this. Maybe taking the cue, she headed out.

Its been a while that I have been feeling uncomfortable around SIRA. The fact that I hate things like 'her' was a well-known fact and just because of that even my daughter was quick to dismiss my feelings.

'Papa, these things are harmless. They have been tried and tested for a decent amount of time now.' It was during one of my ranting cum complaining sessions to her about SIRA. She had dropped in to visit me on her way to a client meeting.

'I have one too and it's a blessing in disguise.' she continued.

She had one way before me. I shook my head. She saw me being silent and asked, 'What is bothering you, Papa?'

I told her then.

For some time now I had been having a feeling that intensified over days and months about how SIRA seemed to be so different. She looked more confident, stronger and something else I couldn't exactly put my finger on. There were also times I felt she was *sneaking* upon me.

When I am on my chats or phone calls, I find her in the same room without any rhyme or reason; mostly on the pretense of cleaning, brining my tea or something else. One day I found her crouching outside listening to my conversation. She had an uneasy look to her face. By god, the way they have engineered to make these things look so human!

I had given her a piece of my mind which she brushed off with a sorry and walked away.

The deal-breaker was when one night I woke up startled from a dream to see her standing at my bedroom doorway supposedly staring at me. Her dark figure loomed over the room as I lay still, my heartbeat wild until I saw her leave silently closing the door behind her.

That was the latest incident and it still sends a chill down my spine.

Shradda brushed that off too. I was aghast.

'It must be you feeling so, Pa. Maybe you cried out in your sleep or something and she was just checking on you. You live alone. Had it any vile intentions, it would have executed the same by now. I have been living with one. I had the creeps in the beginning but by now am used to having it around.'

I still wasn't convinced. SIRA seemed more human, more AWARE. But then that had to be me feeling so according to Shradda, more so because SIRA was bought from the same company and through the same means, my daughter got one for her house.

'Oh, I miss having human help around!' I quipped with a lopsided smile. Shradda laughed with me.

I was seated in the living room with Shradda and I was sure I could feel SIRA listening to me from the kitchen.

As days passed, my paranoia just kept increasing. I was working full time on my book and was fully equipped with the same. I rise early and go for a morning walk and come home to read the papers after which I have my tea, breakfast and medication, in that order. I write after that followed by lunch and a small nap before I get up and have some more tea and medication and then write again until it was dinnertime. Dr. Rajan would drop in now and then to check on me and if I was on time with the medicines, he would be okay. He had no other concern other than the fact that I led a rather lonely life, which I did not mind.

It was the same routine over and over again. I was ok with routines. I did not expect much from life other than that.

It was a Tuesday morning when I came home after my walk to find the newspaper on the table with a page in between torn off and without much thinking I knew instantly who did it.

4

'No sir! I did not take out the paper. I just took the same from outside and kept it at your table!'

SIRA was hell bent on trying to prove her innocence to me.

I did not believe her. I am sure she did it but, WHY? These things have learnt to lie!

'I just have to ask my daughter to send me a screenshot of that page and I will know what was in it!' I barked at her.

SIRA looked at me stupefied like that escaped her

thought process. I then realized I should just have kept my mouth shut – what if she blocks that process also somehow?

I took the phone and tried dialing up Shradda. Her phone was switched off. It's switched off most of the times nowadays and the only way to connect is when she calls me back. I tried one more time and then went to take a shower, trying to keep my calm.

I tried to convince myself that this is just a figment of my imagination. The hot shower calmed me down a bit but when I was out of the shower, I could feel my pulses quickening.

I went and switched on my laptop and tried to check the news for that particular day, to try and see if there was something that missed my notice. I sat there for maybe an hour checking but no...nothing. I felt a movement behind me.

It was SIRA with my medication and my tea.

She looked at me mechanically as if trying to conceal whatever they have stitched onto her of any human emotions. She then tried to open her mouth like she wanted to tell me something. There was a look of hurt in her eyes, which quickly disappeared before it was evident. She walked out without uttering a word.

I went to the foyer in my room where she left my medication and looked at it. It was red in color and I wondered what its name was. Dr. Rajan gave the pills directly to SIRA and for a moment I wondered if he was in this too. **'This'** being a very ambiguous term now since I did not know what I feared.

How about skipping this medication?

Oh no, should I do it?

What if the pills are some sorts of drug that is making you sick in some way? Why is SIRA always spying on you? —My mind echoed.

I took it in my hand and looked at it for a long time, unable to decide. A few minutes later I was enjoying my tea, the red pill concealed in my pocket.

5

It was after lunch and when SIRA went to get groceries that I tried calling up Shradda again. I thought of asking Shradda to email the newspaper clipping to me or to come directly and show it to me. I hope she wasn't busy with a client or some other work, which she always is. I then decided to ask her to come home today and to bring my grand kids this time.

I was missing them a lot.

The phone was still switched off. I kept dialing for another few minutes after which I stopped trying. I knew SIRA will be back any minute and I had to get in touch with her but I had no idea where she was.

I decided to call Amit.

His phone was switched off too. Suddenly it sent an alarm to my head. Where the hell are these kids!?

I send them both messages, asking Amit to call me ASAP when he sees the message and to Shradda asking her to come home quickly when she sees my message. I felt for a moment I was getting paranoid. My heartbeat was quickening and my head seemed to ache. I wondered if it was the aftereffects of not taking the pill and for a moment I regretted it.

Is SIRA going cuckoo? Maybe she just needs a small tweak.

That's when it struck me. I decided to call customer care. I had her serial number and other details kept away neatly in one of my lockers. I had to find them though. I went searching for them and found them neatly piled in one of my books folders where I kept such details

'Gotcha!'

I took out all the papers and decided to call customer care from my mobile.

It was a damned machine even at customer care, which asked me to enter the initial details. After I had done the same, I waited, my leg twitching in anticipation. In between, I kept looking out if SIRA was back. She wasn't.

They were unable to match the information and hence my call was directed to a human. At last!

It was a relief to hear a human voice – natural with all its imperfections on the other end.

'Good morning. Welcome to A&N customer care. This is Neeta speaking. How may I help you?

'Hi, my name is Ajit and I had purchased one of your units last year. I want to log a complaint with regards to the same.'

'Sure. May I have the unit number and the serial number please?' She asked

I gave it to her and she asked for a moment while she checked, as I sat nervously waiting for SIRA to walk in any moment.

'It's the SIRA unit, am I right sir?'

'Yes,' I said to her. I could hear her checking and rechecking and then she excused herself as she put me on hold. These things have still not changed and I had to hear boring music for so long that I almost thought of disconnecting the call.

SIRA could be back at any moment.

So what if she was back. What the hell are you scared of?

I tried to remain calm. I am the decision maker here. I will ask them to take SIRA back right now itself if I feel she is a threat.

There was no sign of SIRA, or Neeta.

'Where the hell are you?' I hissed under my breath.

I heard a click on the other side. Neeta was back.

'Sorry to keep you waiting, sir.' She apologized.

'Yes, yes, it's fine.' I said quickly. 'When can you send someone?' I asked.

'Sir, there is some confusion.'

'What? What confusion?' I asked.

'This unit of SIRA is no longer functional. Its been taken off and returned to us 6 months back.'

I heard a movement near the door and turned around to see SIRA standing at the door looking at me.

'What do you mean?' My voice faltered. I could feel my heartbeat quickening.

'This unit has been returned 6 months back and replaced with a new one.'

SIRA looked at me. Her eyes held an emotion I couldn't decipher. Maybe anger. Maybe murder!!

I had to reach out to someone but I could feel my legs turn to water and me losing breath.

The voice on the other end felt like an echo as she continued, 'Sir, it was ordered under your name by Mr. Ram. Hello Sir...?'

I saw SIRA walk towards me and I held up a hand weakly asking her to stay away from me or else I will kill her.

Can I?

The last I saw was SIRA's looming figure over me. Then all went black.

6

I was drifting in and out of dreams and reality.

I was in my fathers lap when we watched a movie about machines taking over the world. A guy was trying to save a bunch of people though a machine later executed him. The machine, when my eyes closed in to the face, turned out to be SIRA! I cried out in anger.

I heard Shradda behind me then. I turned back to see her and Amit. They were asking me not to worry about SIRA but for some reason I knew they were dead. I asked Shradda to run.

'Ram – he is a murderer and he will kill you!' I screamed. She did not believe me and neither did Amit. I was petrified about my children's safety. I asked them to run and run.

I was screaming when I woke up to the dark room.

Someone was sitting on the couch beside my bed. The figure got up and walked towards me. It was Maya. For a moment I couldn't believe my eyes.

'Maya? But...you are dead.'

There were tears in her eyes as she bent towards me and kissed me on my forehead.

'Its going to be all right baby...' She whispered in my ear softly. I could smell her wonderful hair just the way it was when she was alive. It soothed me somehow. She straightened up and started to leave the room

'Wait! Wait, come back...where are you going?!' I called back after her.

But she did not stop neither did she turn back. I called after her, again and again, my calls slowly turning into helpless pleas.

That was just a dream again.

I got up to find myself on the couch to SIRA, or imposter SIRA sitting next to me, looking at me. My head felt heavy.

I was sure of a few things now.

Ram, my son-in-law had purchased this thing, which I assumed to be SIRA, and somehow planted it in my house without my family's knowledge or mine. He definitely had some vile intentions behind it.

Second, my kids were now missing and unreachable and he might have done something to them. But I wasn't ready to accept that yet...not just yet.

A feeling of sadness crept over me.

'Sir, you did not take your medication. I found it in your pocket.' She opened the palm of her hand and there it lay, the red pill staring back at me.

'What do you want SIRA? Do you want to kill me? Is this why you are kept here by my son-in-law?'

For a moment she looked like she was taken aback but she quickly recovered. These damned things are made so smart.

I was calm. I had nothing to lose. I wasn't going to live here scared. She can kill me if she wants to.

They are never programmed to kill humans, Papa. I heard Amit telling me some time ago, I couldn't remember when or why but the moment I remembered it, I felt an unbearable sense of loss.

'I just want to know what you did to my kids? Why am I not able to reach them?' I almost choked on my words. 'They are the only reason I chose to live.'

'I know for sure that you know very well why I can't reach my children.'

SIRA got up and looked at me.

'Sir, Dr. Rajan will be here at any moment. I have called him and also your son-in-law.'

'What about my kids? Why didn't you call them this time?'

She just looked at me, a blank expression on her face.

'Please be calm sir.' She said and got up to leave. This was my moment. I quickly took the heavy oak chair from the side and bought it down on her with all my might. She turned to see it on time and ducked. Like a cat....

I fell with it on to the floor.

Before I knew, SIRA took me up from the floor effortlessly. I struggled with her to get free but I was nothing in front of her. The miracle shot or not, I wasn't strong enough for her. She plucked me up like a flower from the floor, carried me to the bed like a pro and held me down. I fought with her, kicking and trying to pry her off my shoulders but I couldn't even budge. I could feel my energy draining fighting her off and was almost about to give up when I saw Ram and Dr. Rajan enter the room and I felt my rage increase ten-fold.

'I will kill you, Ram! I will kill all of you! And I never expected you to be in this doctor!' I shouted at Dr. Rajan and Ram.

SIRA tied me down with bondages that suddenly appeared on all sides of my bed. How come I never saw them before? I saw Dr. Rajan rush to the side of my bed. I threw cuss words at him as he took out some medication from his bag.

I felt a cold prick on my hand as I struggled. I was still swearing when I passed out.

7

The next day morning I woke up feeling nauseated and with almost no energy. A few hours later, Ram was back again with Dr. Rajan. Whatever they had pricked me with had kept me drowsy and I was left with no energy to fight. I think its time they told me their motives. SIRA brought me the medication in the morning which she tried to force down my mouth and which I spat on her face. I wasn't tied down anymore. Maybe she expected me to realize that I am not at all strong for her which was true. She could crush me to death before I would even know.

Ram and Dr. Rajan came and sat in front of me. I was seated on the couch again. I looked at them with anger and sadness.

'What did you do to my kid's, Ram?' I asked again.

He was silent and avoided my eyes.

Dr. Rajan spoke up.

'Ajit, I want you to listen to what we have to say with a calm mind.'

He stopped for a while, observing me. Ram looked a bit nervous.

'What the HELL...do you want from me?' I looked at him pointedly

'Amit and Shradda...Amit and Shradda...'Dr Rajan looked like he couldn't complete his words. He pulled out a sheet of paper and handed it over to me.

I saw that it was the same sheet that was torn from my newspaper the day before.

I scanned the paper. At first it did not hit me until I read it again, my bowels turning to water.

6 months since tragedy claimed our beloved star!

I read the article again and again unable to believe it; my head slowly swaying in extreme grief. I saw the names Amit and Shradda. I saw the names of my grand children. The car they were in got into a grisly accident.

The kids died on the spot along with the driver who was Amit. Shradda died on way to the hospital.

Dr Rajan and Ram looked at me pensively as if they expected me to do something drastic at any moment now but I couldn't. I knew I couldn't because my body did not allow me.

'You are lying...' I murmured to them.

I read the article once again. The date the accident had occurred was 6 months back.

'What is all this Rajan?' I asked trying to be calm and trying to show them I can't be fooled. 'What are you trying to prove?'

'Exactly six months back Ajit; you had called up Shradda and asked her to come home immediately. You were paranoid about your help in the house 'SIRA'. You had stopped taking the medications of the miracle shot, which had started inducing in you some sort of mild paranoia, and all your delusions were about SIRA. You thought she was plotting to kill you.' Dr. Rajan's voice was now emotionless.

'That particular day you were convinced that SIRA was outside your room with a knife in her hand, trying to kill you. Amit was at home with Shradda when you made the call and he decided to accompany Shradda to come and see you. They also decided to take the kids with them because they thought that might help you calm down. Shradda had informed Ram about this before leaving home and asked him to come and pick up the kids the next day since it was his turn to take the kids. Amit called you on the way and convinced you that it was all your feeling and that there is nothing to fear.'

After that all I heard was silence. It was as if a rusted tap had suddenly started pouring water and that water started to burn my heart.

'They are never programmed to kill humans, Papa. Many people in my industry use them and they are super safe. You can trust them better than humans!' Amit laughed.

'I am bringing the kids along with me papa.' Shradda had shouted into the speaker too.

That had sent a calming feeling to my heart then and I had decided to come out of my hiding place in the cupboard where I was supposedly hiding from SIRA.

'I believe they were on call with you when the accident happened.' Dr. Rajan's voice cut through my thoughts.

'Yes, they were...' I mumbled

SIRA had opened the door of the cupboard where I was hiding and I had screamed with that damn phone in my hand with my kids listening to me. Even when she tried to calm me down, I just screamed because I was just not taking the fucking medication for a week...which my now dead daughter wanted me to take to keep me alive.

'Amit, we believe, lost focus for a moment that he did not see an oncoming truck while taking the turn and the crash happened.' Continued Dr. Rajan.

'You are right....' I said. 'I remember everything. He was on phone with me when it happened. The phone had got disconnected in between.' I said, lost.

I felt nothing. Just emptiness.

Ram started sobbing.

'When you came to know of the news, you were a bit *too* ok. You were ok until after the funeral and for a week after that, until Ram came home one day to find you in a pool of blood and SIRA damaged and unmoving in another room. You had bludgeoned SIRA and then tried killing yourself. He saved you by taking you to the hospital in time. But you were not ok. You blamed yourself for what happened. You were extremely depressed and suicidal. We realized then that you hadn't taken your medications for almost a week and that is what had induced the paranoia in the first place – the miracle shots side effect.' Dr. Rajan explained

'The miracle shot side effects were a badly kept secret of the product. People knew about it but were still ready to invest in it because they wanted to live. Mortality over common sense. They just had to take the pills regularly to ensure that they were ok and mostly it took a few days before the side effects started showing incase you did not take the pill'

I couldn't bring myself to believe any of this... Extreme grief took over me.

'Why...why am I here then? Are you trying to take revenge on me Ram, for supporting my daughter with the divorce? What use is my life? I was about to die. I extended this just for my kids.' I looked at him with sadness and anger.

'I never blamed you for anything Papa. What happened, was between me and Shradda and I hold only myself responsible for it. I had momentarily wandered off but she was my one true love and I realized that quickly once I lost her. I was begging her to give our marriage another try. I had convinced her that I had changed and that I cannot live without her. She just wasn't sure you would take it in a good way and had asked me for some more time to think it over again.'

'Why the hell am I ALIVE then?!' I shouted in extreme anguish.

'I just want to die. I just want to DIE. I can't live without my family. I don't trust you, Ram. I don't!! Why did the company inform me then that SIRA was returned 6 months ago?' I pleaded to know.

Ram was silent. He looked at Dr. Rajan helplessly.

'Ajit...we can't allow you to die. You are not allowed to.'

'What the hell...who are you to decide that?'

'We are nobody to decide that. But the miracle shot..there are only a certain amount of shots produced a year in each country. Since Amit was famous and influential, he managed to get that shot for you. You won it for yourself while thousand others who couldn't manage it and maybe who even deserved it more had to die. You killing yourself is like spitting on those people who died because you got the medicine over them. We can't allow that and neither will you be allowed to'

'I don't CARE!' I shouted at this bullshit.

'You have to Ajit. This is beyond Ram or me now. The government is involved too. In fact, they keep a tab on all the people who have taken the shots – especially the ones that turn rogue. They won't allow you to die. SIRA here is the eyes of the government. The old SIRA was returned since you had damaged her in your rage. The one in your house is a superior version of SIRA for suicide prevention and care (SPAC). She is here to take care of you and above all to keep a watch on you – a suicide watch.' Dr. Rajan continued.

I fell silent for a moment before I started to laugh. This is insane. I was losing my mind. I couldn't control the laughter that erupted through me. I laughed until tears started rolling down my eyes.

Ram and Dr.Rajan looked at each other helplessly.

I then started sobbing.

I couldn't take this. The pain of cancer was much better than this. At least it was physical. I felt the cancer was now on my heart and my throat, nibbling at it slowly.

I just wanted to die...oh god.

'But people around me, act so normal. I mean I never even got an inkling of this happening to me... I even spoke to Amit and Shradda so many times in the last couple of months', I felt so confused and for some reason, I could recall now only a few conversations I had with them.

'Ajit, you had undergone a severe trauma of losing your loved ones and were extremely depressed and suicidal, coupled with paranoia because of skipping your miracle shot medications. As part of the treatment, we ensured you woke up with those memories suppressed. Right now, you are still on treatment and the world you see around you once you step out, which you rarely do, that is half created holographic illusions to restore your sense of normalcy. As with regards to you talking to Amit and Shradda, those are induced hallucinations. Your mind is just trying to get used to the trauma and we were helping in the process. The medications were mixed with your food and given to you so that you don't get suspicious.

We ensured no news of the tragedy reaches your ears. Your neighbors or anyone doesn't dare speak to you about what happened because everyone is aware of what happened to you and the treatment you are going through. Everyone is aware that SIRA has her eyes on them as well.' Dr. Rajan explained calmly.

'What are you saying Rajan? I can't believe any of this.' I whispered

'Like I mentioned, the government has its eyes on you. We had to put SIRA in place once you tried to take your life. You have to cooperate with us Ajit. She is much stronger than you can imagine and more *aware.* If you try to take your life again... I can assure you that it will be a failed attempt and an unnecessary complication and pain for you...'

I shook my head. I can't do this. I could feel the madness creep upon me.

'How much longer?' I pleaded

'This medicine will work on your body for the next 10 years at least.'

10 years!!! I wanted to strangle him.

'After that, we don't know. Once the effects wear out it depends on your luck how long you will live.' He looked sorry to tell me that.

'For 10 years, SIRA will be with you, watching your every move, keeping an eye on you.'

Trapped. That's the word that came to my mind.

I looked at them as they stood up to take their leave. Ram looked very upset.

'Be strong Ajit. We are here for you...be strong.' Rajan said with a hint of sadness in his voice. He left the room. Ram stood there for a while as if comprehending what to tell me.

'Papa...You are not alone... I am there for you. You can always be in touch with me.' He said and left the room.

SIRA stood there looking pensive. She looked at me and then left the room along with the others.

8

It's been 200 days today since the day I learned the truth of my life. It shattered me enough to make me empty. I was still on suicide watch though they slowly took me off the induced hallucinations. The pills they gave me mixed up with food had induced hallucinations of the good sort as Dr. Rajan had explained so that I don't crack up again and try to empty a barrel of bullets into my mouth. But I didn't try. I did not want the hallucinations. I wanted to be in the real thing...I wanted to feel the pain and rawness of it all. The pain of being a mortal who is now like an immortal. After much hesitation and convincing, Dr. Rajan had finally agreed to take me off the meds.

'If ever you change your mind, Sir, we can start it again.' SIRA told me as she bought me my afternoon tea and found me staring into nothingness.

'Oh ...I have memories SIRA. Real memories and those are what I want. Can I ask you something SIRA?'

'Yes, Sir....'

'Do you mind if I called you Shradda? It will help me a lot.'

She nodded before walking away. In my darkness, I had to find my light – the light of sanity as I waited for death with bated breath.

The Game

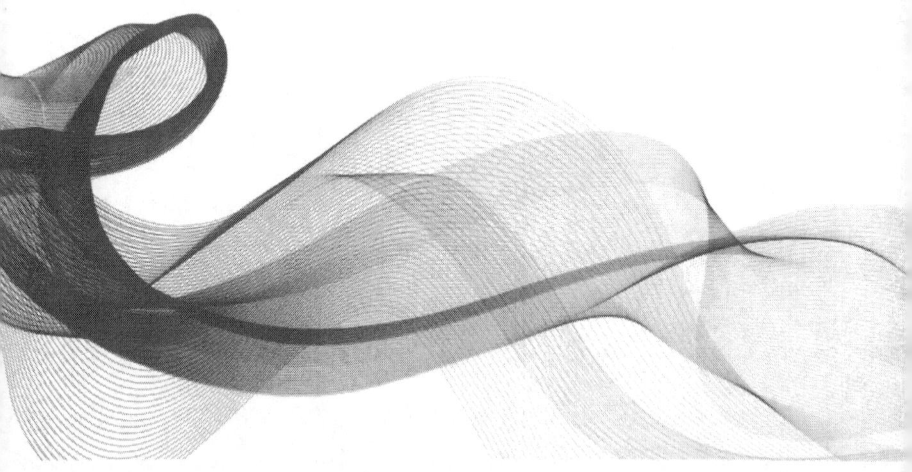

Seth Malhotra was considered extremely lucky and lucky he was if you wanted to know. He knew it too and cherished it in a sly way. In front of you he will behave humble and dismiss all his good fortune and behind your back, his heart rises as he goes over each compliment one by one, relishing it like a sip of hot tea on a cold beautiful morning.

At 30, he was the VP of a leading IT company. He had a beautiful girlfriend Aditi, who considered him her hero. He is planning to propose to her under the Eiffel tower this valentine's day. His parents, friends and colleagues love him – who wouldn't? He had the most amazing smile and the friendliest face. Whether he was genuine or not, no one cared. Everyone wanted to be Seth's friend.

This was until the day he met the stranger.

Seth always enjoyed the two-hour road trip he took once a week going from his current city Dubai to Abu Dhabi for client meetings. He would leave in the morning, enjoy the ride, have a paratha omelet in between – his favorite breakfast and sing to his favorite Bollywood songs as he rode on. When the day got over and the sun went down, he drove back again with a heapful of Bollywood songs to relish and enjoying a hot cup of chai he would get at one of the gas stations.

That particular day as he drove back home after getting his regular cup of chai from the gas station, a phone call distracted him and he took a wrong turn. It was an ad call. He said his *hello* to receive a deathly silence at the other end until a voice suddenly boomed giving him a jump

Do you consider yourself lucky? Do you think you have the guts to invest in. ..

The recorded voice on the other end of the line was loud. Seth cut it off immediately, feeling irritated. He hated these ad calls. The volume was so high that he felt a slight ringing in his right ear even now. A few seconds later he realized that he took a wrong turn and was on the wrong road.

'Dammit!' He hit the steering wheel softly in frustration. He was going to be late now. The ringing in his ear stopped.

Usually taking a wrong turn wasn't a big deal on this highway (he has never taken a wrong turn though, maybe once). Seth always used to find the correct exit to take him back but not on that particular day. He kept driving for a very long time looking for an exit and the more he drove, the more he found just desert on both sides of the road. He even started feeling that the road started looking lonelier and the desert on both sides more *un-natural.* Yellowish streetlights greeted the car after every 5 seconds on either side of the road. It was nighttime and he realized that cars never used this road so it was just natural to find it deserted.

That's when he felt a thud on his car and the feeling that the car ran over something. That something had hit his car from the side and he had ran over the same. He had a glimpse of the thing that came flying from the side and his first thought was, 'Is *that a head?'* That was just a passing random thought on Seth's mind to something he did not see clearly and to which he gave no importance because what concerned him now was if it had caused some damage to his new Merc.

He parked the car on the hard shoulder and got out to inspect his car. He loved his car and it was his baby. That's when Seth saw him – the stranger.

He was well dressed and standing beside a fancy car. That's what Seth noticed first – the car. The McLaren car.

Richie Rich guy!

The guy smiled at Seth.

Seth smiled back unsure.

'Can I get a ride buddy? I am stranded.' The stranger spoke first.

'Oh my God! Did you too take a wrong turn or something? I have never been lost when I take this highway!' Seth was relieved to see someone at last.

'Yes. I guess I took a wrong turn. For some reason my phone is not working too.' Replied the stranger.

Seth checked his mobile and realized that what the stranger said was right. There was no service on his phone either. Looks like the stranger's car broke down and he can't even call the recovery service.

'Looks like you are pretty much screwed up! You are lucky I came along. Come on with me. Hop on.' Smiled Seth. His wonderful smile would sure have mesmerized the stranger.

'By the way I am Seth. Nice to meet you!' He extended his hand towards the stranger. He came and shook it smiling.

This guy looks filthy rich. Good to make such contacts!

The stranger walked towards Seth's car and got in.

'Cool car by the way.' Said Seth smiling towards the McLaren car.

'Oh yeah! You are right. What to do?' He shrugged.

They took off then riding into the settling night with no exit in site. There was an uncomfortable silence for sometime before Seth jutted in.

'It's been a while I have taken this road and it looks pretty changed!' Seth said shaking his head in disbelief. The stranger smiled back.

'So, tell me more about yourself.' Seth continued.

The stranger looked at him for some time before he said, 'You sure you really are interested to know about me?'

'Of course, why not?' Said Seth, his award-winning smile back on his face.

'You are not what you seem to be.' Said the stranger

Seth looked at the stranger and for the first time noticed that he had deep green eyes.

'What do you mean?' Asked Seth. On the road, the exit was still nowhere in sight.

'You smile a lot but it doesn't come from your heart.' Said the stranger.

'Ohh...very deep.' Seth joked.

'No, not deep. In fact, you are a very shallow person.' The stranger continued.

Seth's smile fell.

'I see that you are not smiling anymore.' The stranger smiled again. 'Hope I did not offend you.'

'So, where do you want me to drop you?' Seth was back smiling again ignoring the stranger's question.

The stranger did not reply.

'Halloo! I am asking you my friend.' Seth tried to be as pleasant as possible.

'I am not your friend and you know that very well.' The stranger sounded like he disliked it very much.

He was slowly starting to get on Seth's nerves. The guy was stranded on a deserted road with his fancy car broken and no service on his phone. What would have the moron done had he, the friendly Seth Malhotra not come along and offered him a ride!

Bloody Rich people and their bloody attitude. Maybe he should be dropped back on to the road, thought Seth.

He saw a smirk on the strangers face and did not like it.

The fact that the road kept extending with no exit in sight just added to his irritation. There was not another car in sight even now.

'I wonder if I will find the exit to get out of this road.' Seth said aloud.

'Are you scared?' The stranger asked

'Scared? Of what? There is nothing to be scared about. I just want to reach home on time so that I can do other things.'

He wondered why he allowed this man to get into his car. He would have felt much better without him in it.

'Is your girlfriend waiting for you?' the stranger asked

'No, my wife actually' lied Seth. The stranger still had the leer on his face.

'You have no wife.' He said softly.

Seth looked at him and smiled. He was sure it looked fake, 'Of course I do!'

'Why do you lie? I know very well you don't have a wife.' The stranger kept staring at him. Through the corner of his eyes, Seth could see the stare and it made him uncomfortable.

'May I ask what makes you so sure about that?' Seth managed another smile. He did not want to take up an unnecessary argument.

'You don't have a ring, Seth'.

Seth laughed out loud. 'You caught me there!' Seth realized he was feeling nervous until then.

That stare.

For some reason it got him thinking about serial killers.

What was this guy doing anyway on this secluded road? A rich guy like him?

Can't a rich guy be stranded, Seth? His inner voice admonished him.

The streetlights on either side of the road suddenly started appearing dimmer. Seth felt there were just him, the car and the stranger inside the car driving in the middle of the desert.

He looked at his phone to see if there was any connection. None. This has never happened to him in this part of the world before. There should have been an exit somewhere by now! Something else bothered him now. Aditi. He was planning to drop in at her house and surprise her. It's been a week they met. His work had kept him busy. A nagging thought suddenly found itself in his head, a thought that he had purposely buried deep and ignored. A friend of his had seen Aditi with another guy at a coffee shop. Seth had dismissed it off as some random friend of Aditi's but his friend was adamant. 'They were sitting too close for comfort and their body language too wasn't very. ...friendship types.' his friend had told him.

'Are you hungry?' The stranger asked out of the blue.

'I am too tensed to be hungry.' Replied Seth even though he was indeed feeling hungry.

'What's bothering you then? You look lost.'

Seth wanted to ignore the question but he did not like the look of the guy sitting next to him. He suddenly realized he did not know the strangers name.

'I was wondering what is your name?' Replied Seth.

'Better still you should be wondering what your girlfriend is up to now.' He had that look on his face that made Seth want to stop the car, take him out and beat the shit out of him.

The stranger did not wait for him to answer. 'Beating me up won't solve your problems, Seth.' His voice was low.

The car came to a screeching halt. Seth forgot all about the fact he couldn't find his way home or the fact that his girlfriend must be cheating on him. Seth now felt something new. He could feel the first pangs of fear. If it was someone else, he wouldn't have minded it but the stranger next to him was already starting to give him an uneasy feeling.

They sat in silence now. Seth could hear his heart beat. He looked at the stranger to find him staring out of the windshield.

A smile slowly formed on the strangers face now, a creepy one according to Seth.

'Why did you stop? We have to find our way out Seth. It's already getting late.' The stranger looked amused.

'Why? Why did you say that beating you up won't solve my problems?' Seth asked him cautiously

'Oh that! Many a times people have told me they want to beat the shit out of me when they see my face...maybe it's the way I look. I imagined you must be thinking the same because you had that look on your face...' He still looked very amused.

Seth relaxed a bit now.

'Listen buddy, please can you stop telling me about what you think and about what I am thinking?' The relief was very evident in his voice.

The stranger agreed and Seth gave a big sigh before starting the car again. The car took some time to start. Seth started driving looking straight ahead. He was no more thinking about the missing exit, the dimming lights or about what Aditi was up to at the moment. There were other things on his mind. The stranger next to him still bothered him in an unexplainable way. Those green eyes, the way he smiled, the clothes too perfect and something else, which he couldn't put his finger to.

The creepy smile was back on the strangers face again. It felt and looked as if the stranger was reading Seth's thoughts and smiling.

Seth wondered if he was reading his thoughts or was it the man just had a weird smile that made people feel terrible? Why wouldn't a man introduce himself or give his name.

'A perfect setting for someone to be kidnapped, don't you think?' The stranger suddenly spoke again.

The statement shook Seth up from his reverie

'What a statement to make?' Seth laughed nervously.

The stranger did not utter a word.

'Haven't you done that Seth? Haven't you kind of kidnapped someone? Your best friend?' The voice was low and judgmental.

The car came to a screeching halt again. Seth found himself losing breath.

'What?' Asked Seth. His voice a mere whisper.

'Your friend Siddarth. You thought no one would know and maybe no one does. But you are a work of evil behind that friendly façade.' The stranger smiled at him, pure creepiness emanating from him.

Seth found himself shouting at the stranger with his heart pounding, 'Who the hell are you? What the hell are you saying, man? Who is giving you all this wrong information?'

Seth then realized the growing darkness around them and for a moment wondered if it was the ghost of his friend in front of him. His best friend Siddarth. His best friend that he had indeed...

'Murdered.' The stranger completed his thoughts aloud.

This can't be.

Suddenly he could hear Siddharth's pleas looming large and phantom like on his mind. He could hear Siddarth asking him to spare his life.

'You still remember it, don't you?' The stranger continued.

It occurred to Seth then what was amiss about his person that sat beside him .He never blinked – not even once and his skin was too smooth, like an eggshell. The air inside the car suddenly shifted and felt suffocating.

Seth found himself gasping for breath. He opened the door of his car, stumbled and fell out on the road. He raised himself up by his waist, wheezing and slowly crawled to the side of the road and fell on the sand. He could taste the hot sand in his mouth.

I must be dreaming. This is just a dream. They put something in that tea I had at the customer place and I am hallucinating.

He got up slowly and tried to run but he couldn't. He turned to find the stranger beside him and gave an involuntary scream.

'Why are you upset Seth? Did I say something wrong?'

'Who are you and what do you want?' He whispered, since he couldn't breathe for the life of him.

The stranger smiled again. He stood there with his alien like human face and smiled at him. He now told Seth what he wanted. Seth tried to contain his scream. He screamed like he had never done before and it struck him that he could die screaming. In between he tried telling the stranger that it wasn't his fault. It was she. Aditi. That wretched woman. She had lured him all the while. He is a man after all, isn't he? All those secret touches, kisses, secret messages and declarations of love. Seth always knew women were attracted to him because of his looks and the way he talked and when such an attractive and sexy woman tried to get his attention, he was a human after all. What could he have done? And, he gave in knowing very well she was Siddhartha's fiancé.

The stranger smiled and Seth felt he saw teeth – very sharp teeth. There seemed to be many of them in that small hollow of his mouth than what he showed. It sent a chill to Seth's soul. The chill he did not feel while planning the murder with Aditi.

The chill that he did not feel when he took his friend to that remote field near his city in Mumbai, bludgeoned and strangled him to death, all the while when Siddarth pleaded to him to let him go and even asked him what had he done wrong. He made it look like it was a burglary gone wrong.

The chill he did not feel when he called Aditi after that and told her that Siddarth is no more and they can be together now.

The way he considered himself lucky when no foul play was detected.

'Sometimes humans amaze me with the things they do for love...for lust. Your spine was as cold as steel when you threw your friendship, trust and everything out the window and yet now, here you are shivering like a lost puppy in my presence. And then you call a total stranger like me your friend!' The stranger snickered.

'I regret it. Please believe me.' Seth pleaded knowing very well it will do him no good.

'Yes, you do. I know that. At this moment you really do.' The stranger smiled again and this time Seth was sure about those teeth. Tears ran down his eyes as he tried to scream, his mouth open wide with no sound coming out of it.

His vision slowly dimmed. Then he felt it – a piercing pain on the back of his spine. He screamed now.

Somewhere in his brain and in the thoughts that were soon sucking out of him like into a vortex, he remembered what the stranger had told him. He, Seth, was in a bubble. A sort of pocket in time was created to trap him. The man that stood in front of him was not a man but a creature, an alien from out of this world.

A creature with the skin of a human on top of him. A human he had trapped before him. He remembered the McLaren car.

They come in groups. It was a game for them. They come once in a while from a planet in another Galaxy–these highly intelligent, telepathic beings looking for a few baits. They were the odd ones out in their planet with a craving for sadism and so they go outside their planet looking for preys to hunt and have fun with. It was like a hunting game for them.

Seth was one among the chosen this time. They were watching him all the time. Once they chose their victims, they trap them in a time bubble and play with them and their feelings until they kill them and take their body to move on to the next. It gave them the same level of pleasure as an orgasm for a human being.

He heard the creature laughing now. It was as if the devil himself stood before him and laughed.

'We chose only those who we feel deserve this. We don't harm everyone Seth!'

The pain was now unbearable as he writhed on the sand. Seth wished he died.

'No one will ever find you or your car. No one! Now let's begin. Shall we!'

Seth screamed loudly into the night.

2

Aditi was getting ready for bed. She had cleaned her face and removed the last traces of makeup from her face. She had had a quick meeting with an old friend. She knew him from school and they were just friends. Today, he heads a multi million dollar company in the US. She remembers feeling a slight ache in her heart when she came to know about it. He is grown handsome too. What's worse, he seems *very* interested in her. She never stopped the advances and always met him whenever she got the chance.

Maybe I should dump Seth but its too early for anything.

She looked at her phone as she applied her night cream on her face. She was waiting for Seth's call. She had called Seth a couple of times today but to no avail and she wondered where he was. Maybe he did reach home already and slept off or maybe he was with friends but still, he never failed to call by this time. That was not like him.

Off late he has also been acting smug or so she thought. It felt like success had hit his head. Many a times she did feel slightly hurt by certain comments of his towards her when they are with friends or even otherwise, though he later told her that he never meant anything mean, that it was unintentional and sometimes he used to brush it off as a silly joke. He used to laugh and hug her telling her she was thinking too much and that used to solve it all.

But now there was one more man occupying her head- a very good one that is getting her to becoming less tolerant to Seth's wayward jokes and comments.

That's when the doorbell rang.

She opened the door to find Seth standing there and it surprised her. That was not like him either. He looked tired and there were bags under his eyes.

'Seth!! I never expected you to come today!' She hugged him tight. He did not hug back at first but later, as if remembering it to be the protocol, he hugged her back.

'Can I stay here today?' He asked.

She looked at him. Something nagged her at the back of her head.

'Of course, you can stay here if you want.' She replied.

He then smiled at her. He looked like he could sleep off any moment. He walked past her inside, without saying another word.

She gave him a long hard look before closing the door with a huge sigh. She was just tired and wasn't expecting him at this time and she was imagining too much.

He felt too cold when she hugged him – almost like she was hugging a dead body. That was the last thought in her mind when she closed the door behind her.

The Dreamcatcher

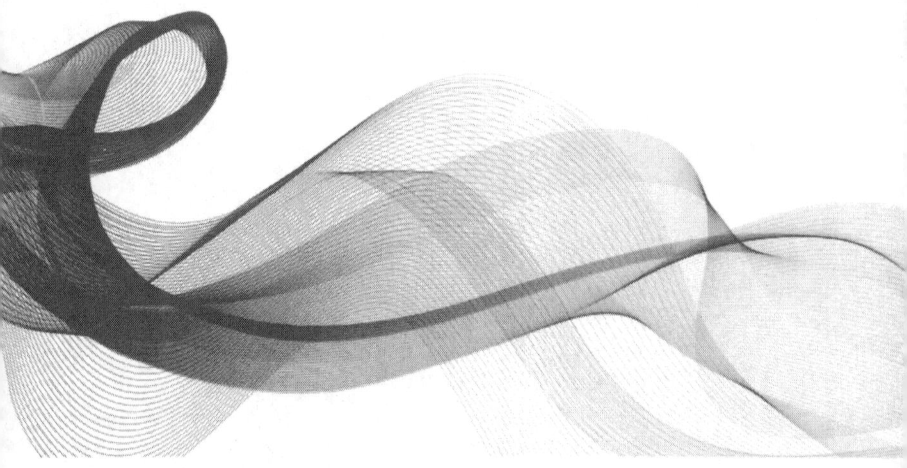

Aishwarya

They say I am a very luck girl and lucky I was.

A baby girl was born to my parents Mr. and Mrs. Sarath. She was named Aishwarya because my parents felt that the baby bought them prosperity and wealth with her birth. Being their only child, they showered her with lots of love and took care of all her wishes.

Aishwarya grew up and became me – beautiful, intelligent, and kind; this is what everyone considered her to be. She excelled in studies, made a lot of friends and even managed to start her own business which was on the way to becoming very successful. She also fell in love and like a dream come true, her first and only love proposed to her and everyone was ecstatic about it including her. She was going to get married to the love of her life.

Everything was perfect until she received a very innocent gift. After that, it all changed for her.

1

'You better come down again for the wedding, Aarti. There are no two ways about it.' Aishwarya looked at Aarti who was busy gulping down the mango pudding made by her mom.

Aarti, her cousin who had left for the US two years ago was back for a short vacation.

'I love everything your mom makes!' Replied Aarti, without looking at Aishwarya. She had picked up a slight American accent which Aishwarya absolutely adored.

'Eat less. You are becoming fat!' Quipped Ash, as her close friends and family called her.

'Yeah, yeah, everyone is not as lucky as you to have such a

great body after eating all the junk!'

Aishwarya laughed at that. She was happy to see Aarti after a very long time. They had grown up together and both of them knew each other like the back of their hands.

They talked and laughed a lot that day, sitting in Ash's room. There was a lot of catching up to do even though they communicated regularly on Whatsapp. They spoke about their childhood, the different guys they met during their teenage, the guys Aarti dated and is currently dating back in the US and also about the upcoming wedding.

'I really want you to be there at the wedding, Aarti.' Ash looked at Aarti waiting to see her reaction. She really loved her and wanted her cousin who is also her best friend to be around on the most important day of her life.

'I will definitely try and I will definitely come. Don't worry!' Aarti smiled and hugged her tight.

When she was about to leave, Aarti gave a slight gasp.

'I almost forgot. I bought a small gift for you, Ash! It's in the car.' She opened the back door of the car and pulled out a medium sized box and gave it to Ash.

Ash opened the box to first see the colorful feathers. They looked bright in the sunlight outside. There were red, black and white feathers. The red ones stood out the most. She pulled them out of the box. It was a *dream-catcher.*[1]

'Wow, it's a beauty!' Smiled Ash. She knew about the dream catcher, though she had never had one. She had seen many of them being sold in street side shops and some fancy shops however she had never thought of buying. The one she held in her hand was very different. Along with its hoop with an intricate web on it and the feathers dangling below, it had a mesmerizing beauty about it.

---

1 ***The dream catcher*** is a talisman that is used to protect people from nightmares and bad dreams

'What do you do with it?' Mrs. Sarath, Ash's mother looked at it admiringly.

'Nothing much. Just hang it above your bed. It catches your nightmares and only allows the good dreams to pass through.' replied Aarti.

'Oh!' Said Mrs. Sarath. It was a dismissive *Oh*.

'Aunty, its not some normal dream catcher. I bought it from a creepy looking old woman who said it's magical.' Laughed Aarti as she got into the car and waved goodbye.

Ash smiled at that but saw that her mother wasn't amused. 'That girl is still the same. She and her lame jokes.'

Later that day Ash sat at a coffee shop waiting for Ryan. The wedding was a few months away and their planning was well underway. The invites have already been sent to relatives and friends. They had been dating for 7 years now and it still feels the same even today – like new love. The diamond ring he proposed her with gleamed on her ring finger. She remembered Aarti looking at it, gasping and then calling her a lucky bitch!

Ryan was an hour late. That was not like him. He wasn't answering her calls either.

Another hour passed. She called him again trying to keep her calm.

Once.

Twice.

Thrice.

The third time a woman answered. For a moment Ash did not recognize the owner of the voice.

'Ash?' It was Ryan's mother.

Ash could feel her calm demeanor slowly trying to collapse – something has happened to Ryan for sure. She wasn't able to gear up a positive thought which was very unlike her.

'Is Ryan ok?' Ash found herself quickly asking.

'Ryan forgot to take his phone, Ash. He left two hours back and told me that he will drop in to meet a friend before meeting you.' Ryan's mother sounded apologetic.

Ash found herself calming down.

What's with you girl?

She disconnected the phone to find Ryan walking into the coffee shop. Her smile lit up the place. She couldn't help thinking that he could have tried calling her from his friends phone to just inform her that he will be late but she pushed that thought away. She was just happy to see him.

They greeted each other with a warm hug. He kissed her on her forehead.

He looked tired and worn out. He smiled but it felt made up.

Something was bothering him. Maybe work was taking its toll on him along with the pressure of the wedding planning. She felt sorry for him though she was going through the same.

'I hope everything is ok? What took so long?' Asked Ash as she ordered two coffees.

'The traffic was bad.' It was evident he was lying.

He did not even bother to say a sorry. Is there another woman? She caught herself thinking and shushed herself up.

Ash told Ryan the details about Aarti's visit and how she really enjoyed spending time with her after such a long time. She realized that Ryan was not paying attention and was looking lost. It was when the coffee arrived that he finally spoke up.

'I thought of not telling and worrying you Ash but you will anyway come to know about it. I almost died today.' Said Ryan softly.

It caught her off-guard and so did the hot coffee. It burnt her tongue and she gasped.

'Are you ok?' Ryan looked concerned.

'Its fine. I ...I did not realize the coffee was hot. Forget about me Ryan. What happened? Are you ok?' She was concerned and upset now. She put her hand over his hand. Suddenly she felt frightened.

She listened calmly as Ryan explained how he forgot to take his mobile. He was supposed to meet a friend but that meeting did not take long – maybe 20 minutes because the friend had to rush to somewhere else. It was while driving to the coffee shop to meet Ash that he realized the phone wasn't with him. For a moment, he wondered if the phone fell down from his lap onto the floor of the car, which often happened with him. It was just for a moment that he ducked down to check if the phone was there (which he agreed was very unwise of him) and did not realize he was jumping a red light.

'I almost got hit by a truck. I missed it by a feather. To add to that, I lost control of my wheel once I realized what had happened and skidded on the road and almost went and hit a pole on the side of the road. It was like I escaped everything by a second...a heartbeat...' His voice trailed off and he went silent again. It was quite obvious that he was shaken.

Ash sat there silent, feeling shocked.

'Ash, I would have died today. I keep thinking about it and can't seem to stop.' He looked frightened.

Ash found herself holding her breath. Slowly she composed herself and got up and walked to his side and hugged him tight.

'Why don't I drop you home and let's forget all about this. I think you need some rest.' She kissed him on his cheek.

She drove him home. They remained silent throughout the ride. Ryan obviously was very shaken and Ash did not try to prod further or ask more questions about the accident purposely. Once she dropped him, she stayed for sometime talking to his mother. By the time she left, Ryan was back to his normal self. But she wasn't. She still needed time to feel ok. Ryan had left his car near a mall and taken a cab after the incident. It had taken him sometime to even drive himself to the mall, which was very close to the accident site. He did not call the police since there was no damage to his car or any other motorist, she remembered him saying the same. She realized that all the time she was thanking God he was safe and there were tears in her eyes.

I missed it by a feather

It kept playing in her head while she entered her home, met her parents, took a bath and even till she had dinner later that night. By the time she was ready to go to bed, she was back to her normal self. It was when she was about to turn off the lights that she noticed the dream catcher. She had forgotten all about it and that she had hung it near her window, near her bed. She switched off the lights. The feathers seemed to gleam in the moonlight and she looked at it for a long time before drifting off to sleep.

2

She dreamt about a very beautiful old woman. The old woman carried in her hand the dream -catcher. Covered in white, with hair that was snowy white and plaited on both sides, she looked at Ash.

'One by one the feathers will fall; your luck will eventually fail...,' the old woman smiled. It was a sinister smile. She was no longer beautiful now. Her eyes were open in surprise, her lips curled in a deathly grimace, her whole skin looked dry and burnt up now as she slowly started pulling the feathers from the dream-catcher one by one with skeletal fingers.

'One by one...they will fall...'

It wasn't a good way to wake up. She got up to see the dream-catcher with the sunlight playing on it.

'Looks like you did not do your job of catching my dreams!' She said it aloud and smirked at the thought of it.

It was while having her breakfast, that she got a phone call. It was Neha calling from her office.

'Ash, there was a fire last night.' Ash found her heart sinking as if she knew what was coming next.

'Our warehouse would have gotten alight had it not been for Sanjay.' Ash got up from her chair almost toppling her cup of coffee on to the table. Her parents looked at her in concern.

'He had slept off on his chair because he had taken some medication. The fire started then.'

'And!?'

'Sanjay put it off. Luckily the fire had not done much damage by the time he woke up. There is no major loss. We checked. We were just lucky, Ash. We just got saved from making a huge loss of money!'

Missed by a feather, she heard the tape recorder playing in her head.

'I am coming now.' Ash told into the phone.

Aishwarya had started her online clothing business three years back and had put a small team together which included old school friends and ex-colleagues and a few others whom she found very capable to help her with her business. It had started slow but within a year she managed to break even. From then on, she had only tasted success. The profit grew by bounds and before she even knew, she was making more money than expected.

Her parents were very proud of her and of what she had managed to achieve. She thanked her quick thinking and her inborn business acumen for the same. It had been just a year that she had managed to have her own warehouse for housing her inventory and this was the first incident since then.

She did not know whether to rejoice to the fact that things just got missed by a second, by a feather or a whatever or to feel bad about the unlucky things that life seem to be suddenly throwing her way and missing her.

The feathers danced in the wind and drew her attention as she applied her makeup. There was something about them that mesmerized her. An almost death like beauty. Those feathers. '*Missed by a feather*', she said aloud looking at them.

The feathers danced again in the wind as if happy she noticed them and she found herself staring at it almost trance like before she was back to her senses. Something was amiss about the dream-catcher. She couldn't put her finger to it. She suddenly felt very gloomy.

By the time she reached the warehouse it occurred to her that one of the feathers were missing from the dream-catcher. She struggled to think if it had 6 or 7 feathers in total when she first got it. Maybe it was always missing and she never realized it.

Neha, her good friend-cum-marketing manager was there waiting outside as she drove in.

'So glad to see you Ash!' Neha hugged Ash as she got out. Together, they walked towards the spot where the fire had started.

The spot had a dozen or more charred clothing. Aishwarya bend to inspect it. Sanjay, her warehouse-cum-logistics manager was beside her looking very apologetic about what happened.

'I am not sure what happened Ash! I really am not. I am sorry this happened!'

Ash took a look at Sanjay and his frightened face. He was one of her ex-colleagues in a boring IT firm she once worked for and he knows how Ash is possessive and passionate about her business.

'Cool down Sanjay.' she said softly

'This medicine usually doesn't make me drowsy, so am not sure why I slept off. I was planning to leave at the same time I leave everyday and...'

'And?' Aishwarya looked at him

'.. Only Dinesh *bhai* was around and I asked him to leave for the day.' Dinesh was one of the two workers in the warehouse who reported to Sanjay.

'Once he left, I received a call from my mother. I was with her on phone for about 10 minutes when I suddenly felt very drowsy and so I finished the call quickly and decided to close my eyes for a few seconds before driving back home. However, I guess I fell into a deep sleep.'

'The fire started with a cigarette, Ash. Someone had carelessly thrown it onto the clothing.' Neha added in.

'How did you wake up?' Ash asked casually as she bent down to inspect more.

'I... I had a weird dream ...'

She had to hold Sanjay responsible for it. He had two men under him and as far as she knew, all three of them smoked. It could have been any one of them who had carelessly thrown a butt into the inventory.

She immediately called for a formal meeting with all three of them and Neha, and issued a strict warning against repeating such a mistake. She also put up a rule of 'no smoking' within the premises.

'I hope you understand Sanjay that I have worked very hard to see it all go in flames.' Ash told Sanjay later that day.

'I totally understand Ash. You don't have to feel bad about it.' He was empathetic.

'So what is this weird dream that woke you up?' She tried to change the subject with a smile

'Oh it really was a weird dream. There was some old lady with a thing in her hand. I think it was a dream-catcher. I have seen those things in some fancy shops...' Sanjay was shaking his head like he was asked to recite a fairy tale and sure that Aishwarya would laugh at him.

But it was like someone had hit her underbelly when she heard that. She felt a lump in her throat.

'Are you ok, Ash? You look like you saw a ghost.' One look at Ash and Sanjay looked concerned.

Ash took a deep breath and tried to compose herself. She tried to smile, to conceal her emotions.

'Why did you find it so weird...the dream?'

'Well, because once I saw that lady and that thing in her hand, its like I KNEW that something wrong was going to happen. The woman kept telling something about luck and feathers...I don't remember. I just remember someone was whispering in my ears to wake up. I mean it was kind of spooky than weird because it felt very real...'

Missed by a feather, the words seemed to run over and over in her mind and she felt nauseated.

'You look sick.' Neha was beside Ash. 'Are you ok?'

'Yes...I think I need to go back home. I am ...I think its too much tension for one day.'

That was unlike her.

Neha offered to drive her back but Ash declined. She wanted to organize her thoughts and be alone during the half an hour ride to her house.

Aarti was at the airport waiting to board the plane back to the US when she got the call from Ash. She wanted to know where Aarti had got the dream-catcher from and if the lady really told her it has magical powers.

Aarti laughed aloud at this, 'Ash!! I just made that up to pull your mother's leg. She was so dismissive about the gift.' She tried to make it sound light.

'Oh...ok.' Ash sounded lost.

'Is everything ok, sweetie? You don't sound so good.'

She thought of telling Aarti about Ryan and the warehouse incident but she didn't want to talk about it and chew more into it, which she tended to do when she spoke about her problems to Aarti. Maybe she will tell her about it later.

'I am good! Just that too many things happening and the wedding is also around the corner. I feel I am too stressed out and thinking of too many things.' Ash tried to sound cheerful.

'Just relax dear. Take it easy and don't think too much. Remember how I used to call you a lucky bitch? Guess what? You still are!' They laughed at this.

Even though she had laughed with Aarti, Ash was feeling very gloomy. She was driving back home and was lost in thoughts. She almost bumped into a car when she forgot to put the brakes on time. The car honked at her before driving off. She parked the car on the side of the road and tried to calm herself down. She tried counting all the way back to 1 from 100, taking small deep breaths and once she felt she was ok, she took the car to the road.

'I am just thinking too much.' She told herself aloud in the car

What are you thinking too much about though?

'The dream-catcher...it has...something to it'

What is it and why are you so afraid to say it out loud?

'Because I am a logical person that's why!'

What is it that you want to say?

'The dream catcher seems to be magical like it has some power of its own.'

Now isn't that something!

'Yes and its bothering me because it's the most idiotic thing I have said but at the same time I just can't get over that feeling nagging me at the bottom of my gut!'

Once she said all that out loud she felt a little better. It's all her imagination. The stress of the upcoming wedding, the incident with Ryan and the incident at the warehouse was just stressing her out and her mind is trying to come up with conclusions about the same because that's what she always wanted, wasn't it. Order in everything. An explanation to everything.

Outside, the weather seemed dusty and for a moment she felt like she saw some red and white feathers swishing by

I am thinking too much now...way too much.

She switched on the local radio network and tried to concentrate on what the RJ was babbling about but she kept hearing 'feather' in between.

The 'feather' outside is not as great as we expected it to be. 'Feather' it will continue or not the same way is something we ought to wait and watch.

Keep listening to your 'feaaather' radio ....

She switched it off, waited for a few seconds and switched it on again.

It all sounded normal now and she enjoyed the rest of her ride back home.

'You look really tired Ashu. I hope everything is sorted out at the warehouse?' Her mother hugged her.

'All is fine Maa.... Can I get some strong chai?'

'Getting for you right now!' She kissed her and went to the kitchen.

Ash walked into the room and closed it behind her feeling relived. The relief was short lived. She looked at the dream-catcher and stood there in disbelief and shock.

It hung there in all its beauty with its white, red and black feathers–minus one more feather.

This time she was sure about it.

3

The nighttime with its dreamscapes was something that Ash had been comfortable with all her life. Not tonight though. She lay awake looking at the dream-catcher. It cast shadows on her face, glowing like a white ghost in the light of the moon. The spider like mesh in its hoop with its tiny beads sparkled or so it seemed to her. For the first time in her life Ash felt scared being alone in her room.

It had taken her sometime to switch off the lights; her logical side fighting with her illogical side. Once she did manage to switch off the lights, she couldn't take her eyes off the dream-catcher.

It's just a dream-catcher.

She sighed.

That afternoon, her mother had returned with tea to find her sitting in the living room looking upset. On asking why she looked upset, Ash had asked her mother if someone was in her room and if anyone had tried taking the dream-catcher off or maybe pulled out the feathers. Her mother had looked at her queerly. She explained to Ash's satisfaction that no one had touched her dream-catcher, not even the maid when she cleaned the room. Her mother was sure about this because she was with her the whole time.

That query was answered yet it was getting tough to wait

for dawn in that room. The only question that loomed large was...*Then where did it go?*

She slowly fell asleep with the thought in her head, exhausted from the day's events.

She got up to the sound of someone's soft laughter in the room.

Even though the initial thought was *it's just a dream*, she heard it again. A slow muffled laugh like someone mocking.

Go back to sleep Ash

It was completely silent in the room. She listened again.

This time nothing.

I am going completely nuts.

The dream-catcher was still there though it was completely dark now.

A movement to the left had her making out a form that seemed to be sitting on top of her study, on the left of her bed. She squinted at it, trying to make sense.

There seemed to be a figure sitting on top of her study...A silhouette of a rather beefy person with long hair, and that's when she realized that she was completely frozen. She couldn't move her hands or her head and she couldn't even breathe. The only part moving were her eyes. She now closed them shut.

She felt cold fingers slowly curling around her neck trying to cut off her lifeline and she knew that the fingers belonged to the figure sitting on her study .The figure she couldn't see but which terrified her soul. She said a prayer she had learnt as a child.

Open your eyes.

She did not open. She kept chanting the prayer, tears flowing from her eyes.

Its all a nightmare.

She could feel her body still paralyzed but now she could

feel a movement close to her.

Open your eyes!

No!

She felt like someone breathing beside her and almost cried out loud. The air around her got heavier by the minute. She did not stop whispering her prayer and kept her eyes tightly shut.

After sometime, the air around her started to get lighter and she felt she could breathe again. It was like someone had got off her chest.

She opened her eyes slowly, half ready to scream and half ready to run.

The room looked as peaceful as it was when she went to sleep. She realized that her bed was wet and that she had let go during her moment of terror.

She lay there still – too scared to move or breathe.

4

'She just had a night terror didi. The upcoming wedding, the incident with Ryan and at the warehouse has stressed her out a lot. That's all.' Ash's aunt, who was a psychiatrist explained to her mother and father.

'She just needs to relax and take it easy.' She continued. Her parents seemed much relieved after hearting that. But not Ash.

In the wee hours of the morning, at the first ray of sunlight, Ash had called out for her mom.

Mrs. Sarath was a proud and happy woman. She was happy with the way her life turned out from the time she was married to Mr. Sarath. In her days, most of the women weren't even allowed to choose their husbands. It was the same for her too. Marrying Mr. Sarath was a boon. Her handsome husband was not just handsome on the outside but also in the inside

– the owner of a beautiful heart. He had considered her his equal and together they had started their business, which later flourished along with the birth of their beautiful daughter Aishwarya.

The blessing did not stop there. Aishwarya grew up to be even smarter and prettier than her mom and as people envied her, they envied her daughter too.

Today however she wasn't ready for what she saw when she walked into Ash' room. Her daughter had urinated in her bed in the night and was sweating profusely and looking distressed. She did not even wait for a minute and had called up her sister who was a psychiatrist.

After her aunt left, Ash's dad looked at her and asked her softly to take a few days off from work. She nodded at that. She loved her work and that kept her happy and feeling alive. To stay away from it was just out of the question. She however decided to take a day off and go and meet Ryan. It's been two days since they had talked. They just communicated on Whatsapp after Ryan's accident. Ash had purposely given him some space.

After calling up Neha and informing her that she is taking the day off, she called up Ryan. The phone kept ringing however he did not answer.

Damn it!

She threw the phone on the bed and paced up and down. Her thoughts were becoming increasingly negative and that was very unlike her.

Why isn't he answering the call?

Before the accident, he used to call her once in the morning and once in the evening. Now even though she purposely had given him some space, she expected him to at least give her a call. She is the one who also initiated the Whatsapp messages for a few days.

She looked at the dream-catcher lazily hanging near her bed and a sort of anger filled her up. She got up on her chair and pulled it down.

'That's it. If I have problems with this thing, am getting rid of it!' She said to herself.

She fetched a matchbox from the kitchen and took the dream-catcher with her to the garden. She threw it in the corner, lit the match and threw it on the dream-catcher. A sort of satisfaction filled her as she saw it slowly catch fire. She walked back to her house feeling like a weight was pulled off her chest.

There, that's taken care of now. I better go and meet Ryan.

As she drove to his work place, she called him again. He did not answer the call. When she reached there, she was informed that he did not come in for work that day and was on a week's leave. She was taken aback with the news since he had not mentioned anything about that to her. She decided to go to Ryan's home to meet him.

Ryan's mom did not seem too happy to see her there.

'He is out with his friend and will be back in an hour. Why don't you come later?' She was uneasy when Ash asked for Ryan.

'Its ok aunty. I will wait.' She said firmly and saw that Ryan's mother did not expect that reply from her. She waited for an hour browsing through magazines and her phone before Ryan walked in. He was surprised to see her waiting for him.

'Ash, what happened?'

'That's what I want to ask you Ryan. What happened? Why are you so aloof?' She did not mean to be so direct like that but she had gotten frustrated waiting for him and with all the holding back of information, she did not care anymore.

She saw Ryan's mother come out of the kitchen where she

was preparing lunch. There was concern in her eyes.

'I am sorry if you felt I am aloof Ash. Let's go to my study and talk.' Ryan told her softly. Ash found herself relaxing at this. Maybe she was just reacting too much to nothing. She walked with him to his study room.

'Did you have coffee or anything?' He asked before settling on the couch that was in the room.

'I am fine. Aunty offered me some when I came but I didn't need anything.'

Ash realized that she couldn't bring herself to ask or tell him anything. She was very upset and expected him to be happier to see her there instead of the way he had behaved, as if he was seeing an ex-colleague.

'I am sorry I did not call you after you informed me about the warehouse incident.' Ryan tried to break the ice. She did not reply to him. She kept staring at the bookshelf in front of her willing herself to talk.

'I understand Ryan. You are still distressed about the accident, I understand. Just that...'

'No am not, Ash.' He replied quickly before she completed her sentence.

'Then? I came to know you are on a week's leave but you never mentioned anything to me. What is happening?' She realized that she was not feeling very good.

'Ash, listen to me carefully. I still love you a lot but I ... I just want some more time.' He said very calmly.

She thought she heard it wrong and looked at him stunned.

'Time for what?' She asked hoping against hope that it wasn't what she thought it was.

'For the marriage. I feel we should...delay it a bit. Listen to me before you get upset.' He said quickly. 'It's the accident.

I was shaken up. You were right but then it got me thinking about my priorities in life right now.' There was a certain pain in his beautiful eyes.

'And?' She asked him, her own heart threatening to break.

'Marriage is not what I want for the time being. In fact I don't know if I want it at all...' He sounded apologetic.

She did not reply. She felt like someone had slapped her tight across her face.

This can't be happening. This just can't be happening.

'Are you calling off the wedding, Ryan? Are you out of your mind?' She whispered to him now. He did not look at her. He did not reply her either.

'After all the invites sent and everyone been told about us... you want to back out?' She questioned him as if questioning his sanity.

'I wasn't sure of how to present this to you and hence I was keeping away from you. I am sorry Ash. Maybe I am just screwed up in the head and it will all just pass and I will realize...', He saw her getting up to leave.

'Ash, I want you to know that I just need some *time.*' He sounded desperate and confused now. He got up quickly and held Ash's hand.

She snatched it away from him.

'Take all the time you want but don't come back to me after that!' She sounded emotionless and walked away from him. She walked out of the room to see Ryan's mother outside, looking apprehensive.

She opened her mouth to say something however Ash did not wait to listen to her and quickly walked outside to her car, got in and drove out from there. She expected Ryan to come behind her but he didn't.

7 years of her life gone. Just like that! It was half way

down the road that the tears she had tried to hold back started blinding her and made her drive almost reckless. She stopped the car, controlled herself and started driving again. It was after she reached home and was alone in her room that she let go and sobbed uncontrollably.

The next two days went by with heated arguments between her parents and Ryan's parents. It was the blame game. Apparently Ryan's parents checked Ash's *Kundli* again and found that she will bring bad luck and even death to her spouse. That led to another round of heated arguments and shouting between them.

These were people who kept their egos and their children above common sense. In normal circumstances, she would have asked her parents to let go but right now she just did not care. Her relationship, which she considered so sacred, had now filtered down to her *Kundli* – that's all it was now for everyone. She wondered if it was the same for Ryan too. She kept getting calls from a concerned Neha asking when she will be back at work. She told her she wouldn't be back for a couple of days and requested her to take care of everything in her absence. Deep inside she felt sad and humiliated as people slowly started to know about the wedding being called off.

'What's happening Ash? This is not you.' Neha sounded very concerned

'I will try to be back soon Neha...it's a family issue.' She said and disconnected the call feeling guilty for neglecting her work.

Ryan tried calling her a time or two but she ignored. There was nothing left to talk. A person who feels his priority has changed after an accident and if she was not in that priority list then it's a red light. A red light to stop everything then and there and to turn routes.

She ate her grief as she dressed up to leave for work after

two days. She just couldn't get herself out of it. This was her first real heartbreak. She never was in a relationship before Ryan and with him everything went well until today and the pain took her by surprise but she tried to be strong. This is what heartbreak felt like. It was like something was eating you alive from the inside as you tried to remain civilized and alive.

'You are a lucky bitch!' She said to the mirror that reflected her face covered in makeup and sobbed. It was like a live nightmare.

The dream-catcher catches nightmares; she found that random thought in her head. She thought about the one she burnt. *Did that one catch nightmares not just in dreams but in life too? Is that what this is all about? That does make sense, doesn't it? I burnt it and is that why now things have started falling apart?*

She remembered the dream with the old woman and what she said in the dream

'One by one the feathers will fall; your luck will eventually fail...'

My luck hangs by a feather? She almost laughed hysterically, amused at that thought.

Why are you laughing Ash? What if it's true – that thing you just thought? What if it's true? Then it's evil, isn't it? Evil because it's controlling your life and your sanity now.

Ash looked at the mirror again. Ever since the dream-catcher was gifted to her, things were going haywire in her life. But it's just a dream-catcher, isn't it and was gifted to her by her cousin who loved her a lot.

She sobbed now uncontrollably at her thoughts. How can she even think all this? She, who was known for her beauty and brains. She, who was known for being very practical and hands-on in life.

Before she left for work, she went and checked the spot

where she had burnt the dream-catcher. It was not completely burnt. One feather was still intact and she found herself indecisive.

No, am not going to allow this to happen to me. I am not taking it back.

She walked to her car and drove to work leaving the half -charred dream-catcher behind. It gleamed in the sunlight.

The day at work passed without incident but Ash realized that she couldn't concentrate on work like before. There were so many thoughts running in her head that it seemed to even block her creativity. She left work early. She remembered the days she used to be the last one to leave and the first one to arrive. It was like her heart was empty and devoid of the passion that drove her life. For a moment she had a bad urge to call Ryan. He always knew how to put her mind at ease. She pushed that thought away and concentrated on the merging traffic ahead.

He called her.

She saw his name flashing and let it go to voice mail. She was confused now. Should she answer his call? Why was he trying to call her? What was left to talk now? That he was still confused about marriage?

The phone lit up again with Ryan's name. He was calling her again. She tried to control her emotions as she answered the call. She took a deep breath before answering the phone.

'Ash…Ash why won't you answer my calls?'

She did not reply to that.

'Ash, I know you are angry. I know you hate me. I just want to talk to you please?'

'What is left to talk, Ryan?' She said softly, trying not to cry. She was so happy to hear his voice again. 7 years of passionate love – how can she forget his presence in her life that quickly? She can't.

'Can we meet at our usual coffee place, please?' He sounded like he was pleading

And then...

'I miss you like hell Ash... I don't know what got over me. It was like someone else was making me say those things I told you. It was like ...it wasn't me Ash. I don't know, this is all messed up.' He sounded like he was in pain.

She felt scared hearing that.

'Let's meet at our usual place. I am almost there. I will wait for you.' She said softly. She had to meet him. Her heart was threatening to explode with the light of hope it saw. The hope of getting back with him again. The hope of things being the way they were before. She was lost without him. Her complete life felt meaningless and in disarray. She always thought it was her work that gave her life – little did she realize that Ryan was also a part of the passion that drove her life. He made her feel invincible.

She reached the coffee place and a sudden nausea overcame her. She was reminded of the last time she had met Ryan here – the look of horror on his face when he told her about the accident he had escaped from. She realized she never visited this place after that. She went in and ordered coffee. She noticed that there were only a few people in there. Some of them were busy on their laptops and some of them on their phones. The place always relaxed her but not today.

She ordered her coffee and waited for Ryan.

An hour passed with no news from him. She had finished her coffee and was contemplating on whether to order a new one.

She looked at the phone willing for it to ring. It didn't. She called him instead. His phone was switched off.

Unease came over her. She could feel the bile rising and felt she might vomit any moment. It was like a déjà vu. The same place, the same table and he was late again- the same way.

Only that this time there is no dream-catcher to help you. No dream-catcher hanging in your room to catch all that nightmares from happening in your life.

A sense of doom washed over her. It was like she was standing at the tip of an abyss and trying hard not to fall down into that darkness. She dialed Ryan's number on her mobile and willed for it to ring. It did not. It was switched off again and she felt herself tipping slowly and slowly over the edge with each call. It was switched off each time she called. This time it wasn't even ringing. His mother was not there at the other end to tell her that he forgot to take his phone and that he was going to be late. She tried to fight back tears as she called him one more time. It was switched off like it never existed. She saw one or two people looking at her maybe noticing her restlessness. She got up slowly and left the coffee place. It was 2 hours now since she had been trying to speak to Ryan.

Maybe he just changed his mind again and switched off the phone because he was ashamed to tell her that.

She was ok with that as long as he is alive and breathing. She was very much ok with that as long as his mangled remains are not picked up from some car crash site. She found herself breaking down at that thought. She got into her car but did not switch it on. She dialed a number again. This time to Ryan's mothers mobile.

She answered it in the second ring.

'Aishwarya, what is it?' She never called her by her full name. That was a first.

'Is Ryan at home?' She asked hopefully.

'No he is not. He was supposed to meet you, wasn't he? He told us today morning that he cannot live without you and what he did to you was all a mistake! Let me tell you something, we are not at all in favor of this like before. We tried making him understand but he won't listen to us!'

'Aunty, he hasn't come to meet me yet. It's been 2 hours since I spoke to him last. His phone is switched off too.' Her voice broke.

There was silence on the other side of the phone.

'What are you saying? What did you do to him now!' It was almost a scream.

She disconnected the phone. She couldn't take it anymore. She called a couple of his friends but they had not seen him either. She then called his colleague to understand that he was still on leave and that they have not seen him for more than a week. She thought of calling the police but then she did not know what to tell them.... that he was missing? Was he missing? She dialed his phone again. It was still switched off. She was in front of her house now. She did not even realize that she had driven there.

It was when she was about to get out of her car, that she received a call from one of Ryan's friend whom she had called earlier. A while later when she opened her mouth to let out the scream that came out of her guts, it stayed inside the car unknown to her parents who were at home watching TV.

5

It was some sort of noise from the outside, Mrs. Sarath had later told her sister, that made her open the curtains of her window and check. She was surprised to find Ash's car outside without her in it. She went out to check for her, a slight unease creeping upon her nerves. Seeing Ash's car without her wasn't something that 'sat well' with Mrs. Sarath. It was some sort of a scratching noise from the garden that made Mrs. Sarath go and check out there. She saw a figure on the ground and for a moment got scared thinking if it was some intruder in their backyard until she recognized her daughter's dress. It was Ash on the ground. When she called out to Ash, she did not first heed to it. Mrs. Sarath called out to her again walking, almost running towards her. By this time Mr. Sarath was also outside checking what was happening.

'She was searching for something when I reached her. I kept calling her but it was like she couldn't hear me.' Mrs. Sarath was trying to keep her tears in check as she spoke to her sister.

'She was murmuring something. She was looking for something. When I tried to hold her, she pushed me back and asked me to stay away and not disturb her.'

Mrs. Sarath remembers catching a glimpse of her daughter's face then. It wasn't the lovely face of her beautiful daughter. It was a crazed person she saw there – a ghost with mud on its face and clothes and hair all disheveled. Mrs. Sarath had suppressed an involuntary cry that had come from her throat. A cry of fright.

'I have to find that dream-catcher. It still has a feather on it!' Ash had almost screamed back at Mrs. Sarath before going back searching for it again on the ground. When she finally did find it, there was a small yelp that she gave like a dog that had found its bone. What Mrs. Sarath saw then in her daughter's eyes was not happiness but adoration- like she worshipped the thing she held in her hand.

Mrs. Sarath had stood there -stunned, afraid to move and her hands shaking, as her daughter sped past her with the dream-catcher in her hands. It looked black in color like it was burnt as Ash carried it like a baby into the house and into her room.

She had then followed Ash into her room calling after her as she came back to her senses, 'Ashu...where are you? What happened to you?' Half crying, half frightened, she had walked into Ash's room. She saw that Mr. Sarath was already there at the door, his eyebrows raised in tension, his lips quivering. What she saw there is something Mrs. Sarath says now to her sister, that she will never be able to forget till the day she dies.

Ash was on her stool and she had already hung the burnt dream-catcher near her bed and now she was taping the remaining feather to the hoop. She kept on turning the tape all around the feather and the hoop like a crazy person. All the while, there was that same glazed look in her eyes, the same look of adoration and fear mixed in them. She looked at it as if she was in a trance.

'Ashu?' Mrs. Sarath had called out to her. It wasn't a call; it was more of a plead.

A plead that actually meant to say 'Please cut this all out and tell us that you were just acting and you were just pulling our leg.' A plead that meant to ask Ash to be the same old person she was – their beautiful loving daughter and that this was all a nightmare.

Once she was satisfied with her work, Ash had looked at her parents and had spoken in a business like tone, 'Now he will be all right. Ryan will be all right. I just have to make sure this feather stays right here.' The business like voice turned to the whimper of a child in despair.

6

It was around 11 pm in the night when a Ford Focus pulled into an old town in a remote area of Texas.

A woman got out of the car and walked towards an almost dilapidated house that was set in well inside the side of the road. It looked spookier than she had imagined. She shivered in the cold wind that unexpectedly blew towards her and she covered herself tighter with her coat. She got to the house and knocked on it hard. It was some time before an old woman well into her 70's opened the door.

'So...it's done?' Asked the old lady sarcastically on recognizing the woman.

'Its cold outside. Can I come inside?' Asked the woman. The old lady hesitated before opening the door to allow the woman to walk in.

The old lady did not like the woman – not at all. She never liked her the first time she met her either. What she asked for was not something she liked doing at all. In fact she had left doing that a long time back after she had given birth to a stillborn. But the money and the deteriorating health of her husband is what made her accept this.

'I only said to ensure her downfall. I did not want to harm the man.' The woman said.

The old lady looked at her with despise. 'She is your best friend, isn't she?'

'Cousin.' Corrected Aarti.

'I have no control over these things. You said downfall and that was ensured – the guy is her weak point so it happened automatically.'

Aarti nodded her head. She felt an unusual chill on her spine standing in that house and for a moment wondered if she was an idiot to be there at 11 pm in the night with a woman who was considered a witch, who practiced witchcraft and black magic. The house smelled of sickness and failure. The old lady looked very sinister and Aarti realized that the lady disliked her. Aarti took out a small bag from her purse and handed it over to her.

'The rest of the money as promised.' Aarti did not look at the old woman's face. She was about to leave the house when the woman spoke behind her.

'Please don't come here again.' It was not a request but a rather chilling warning.

Aarti did not turn to look at the woman, scared that she might see something else. She got out and walked fast to reach her car when she felt something like a hand catch her leg – she screamed and fell down. She turned to look and realized that it was just an extended branch of a small shrub. She got up hastily and walked towards her car. Once she got in, she closed the door quickly. She could now hear the chilly wind around her car. She looked up to the house and for a moment felt she saw the shadow of the old lady standing at the window and staring at her. She started the car and drove out not looking at either side of the road, scared that something might jump out from the dark and on to the car. She never wanted to come back here ever again.

Aarti

My parents happiness were a bit marred when they found out that I was a girl and not a boy when I was pulled out of my mothers womb on the wee hours of a Diwali morning. I have always thus tried to keep up to my parent's expectations so that they were never disappointed in me. My parents were 'blessed' with a baby boy after 4 years but it wasn't with him my parents compared me with. It was with Aishwarya; my uncle's daughter.

We were born the same year and the same month and from the time I was born, my parents and relatives alike compared me with her.

She was beautiful whereas I was just cute. She was talented whereas I had no talent. She was pleasant and always smiling whereas I was always considered grumpy and ungrateful. She was considered lucky for her parents whereas my parents saw me as a burden. She always got what she wanted without much fuss whereas I always had to work hard or to please hard for what I wanted.

'Look at Ash and learn...' My ears had grown numb to hearing this from everyone around me especially my parents.

From the time we were children, she got the best clothes, best toys, the best friends, the best compliments and the best gifts. I would wish for something and the next day I would see it in her hands and feel a pang of jealousy and rage fill up inside me, which I couldn't decipher.

I tagged along with her because I was forced to by my parents and she considered me her best friend. She would tell me about her dreams, her crushes, her everything and I would listen not giving a damn. She thinks she knows me very well but she only saw 'the me' that I showed her. The real me she never knew and never will because that one never really liked her that much.

Later when we were teenagers, guys would want to be with her whereas I had to work hard to get their attention and affection and was considered desperate and needy. All was ok until Ryan came into our lives. He was the deal breaker.

I met him in college (Thankfully, I wasn't with her in the same college). I have never met a guy like him. He was handsome, intelligent and a thorough gentleman. So different from the many guys I have met and gotten used by. He treated me with respect and considered me his good friend. In many ways we shared a bond and I hoped to one day be in a more serious relation with him only to be proven wrong when he met Aishwarya. Once he met her, he was smitten by her. I curse till today the day I introduced her to him.

A part of me thought he would not pursue her further. But he did and before I knew, they were in a relationship.

I was heartbroken. I remember holing myself at home, not eating for days. I told myself that their relationship wouldn't last long–maybe a year or two to put myself out of my misery. They proved me wrong and the relationship just got stronger with every passing year.

I left to the US to pursue further studies and to get away from this mess. I couldn't take it anymore. However I waited for that day when I would get a call from Ash to tell me that she had broken up with Ryan. Something told me they would. Every time a call came from Ash, I would pick up the phone hoping to hear that news. Call she did–one night while I was sleeping and this time I knew he had dumped her because of the ungodly time she was calling me at. She had called me to tell me that he proposed to her and that they were getting married soon. I remember going numb when I heard the news.

I also remember breaking everything in the house after the call. She was so excited. She told me I was the first person she had called to inform after her parents. I hated her so much then.

Aishwarya, my cousin– she was successful, getting married to the guy I loved and was also on the way to becoming rich- and here I was holed up in a small apartment in the US trapped in a job I hated. I just couldn't take it.

I wanted to see her downfall then. All the years of resentment and hate came out like an avalanche and like a crazed woman; I started thinking about how I can bring her downfall. I wanted to see her in pain just the way I was in.

It wasn't a regular dream-catcher that I gifted her. It was poisoned. Poisoned with my hatred towards her and with witchcraft. Once I gifted it to her, I sat back and enjoyed the show. The only thing I did not expect was Ryan to get hurt.

He was on his way to meet Aishwarya when he got into a heated argument with a group of guys when their bike had banged into his car. One thing led to the other and they beat him up and bludgeoned him. He was now in coma. The doctors have no hope.

And Ash...well from what I understood, she is under treatment but won't let go of that dream-catcher. Her business I heard is shut down for the time being since there is no one to take care of it. Her parents are now more concerned about getting their daughter better.

Am I evil? I don't consider myself so. Just a regular human with emotions of jealousy and hatred and I decided to let it get the better of me.

But right now, I feel a sense of loss because now I don't have anyone to compete with. In a way she was the fuel that drove me to do better.

1978

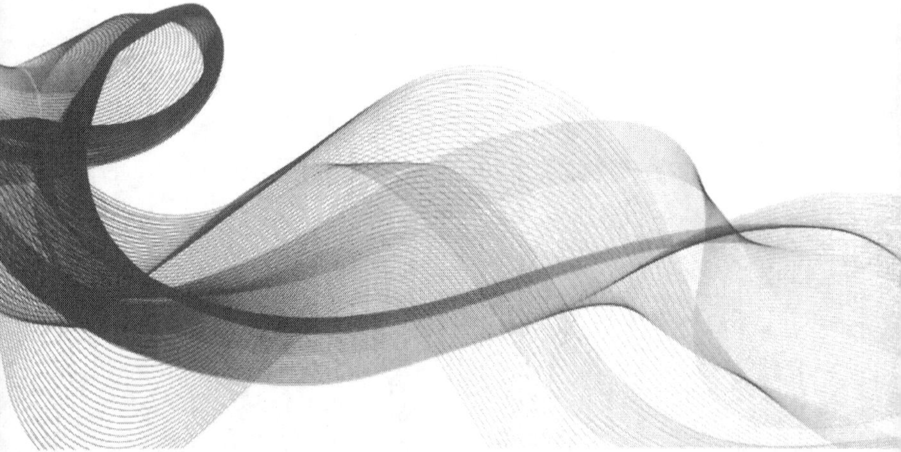

The year was 1978.

You won't believe what happened when I walked down that muddy path on that fateful night. Even today, years later, it gives me the Goosebumps just thinking about it. Till date I never discussed it with my wife or my children. Doing so is like digging up a grave and allowing the stench of the dead overcome my senses- that's the effect it still has on me. There are nights when my wife wakes me up when she hears a muffled scream or a characterless babble from a sleeping me.

'Is it that dream again?' She asks me. I nod at her, a slight sweat forming on my forehead and she leaves me at that. It was an understanding between us. The years and the power to forget has helped me overcome my nightmares eventually. However that night is still clear as crystal to me even today.

The muddy path I talk about ran in between a huge paddy field and on both sides of the narrow path, one could see stretches and stretches of the field; the ends of it bordered by faraway trees and houses with lights that flickered like small fireflies.

I was walking home from my cousin's place and I was late. I was supposed to leave an hour earlier but you know how it is when you meet cousins after a long time. I currently worked in Dubai and was in Kerala for a short vacation. There was a slight wind that night.

The night was slowly turning darker and a chill accompanied it. I could only hear the buzz of the wind in my ears, the grasshoppers chirping occasionally and the unearthly cawing of the crows. I felt goose bumps swell up on my back. The moon that tried to help me with light kept hiding between the monsoon clouds. I had a torch with me that I used to see the path in front of me.

'I should hurry up.' I do not know why I told myself that.

That is when I heard the laughter. Piercing through the cold air and the night that was slowly creeping in, the laughter, which was almost evil had the hair on my back stand in attention. Fear froze my limbs and I found myself immobile for a second. I looked around to see the stretch of paddy fields darker than ever. I couldn't see the trees or the houses at the horizon of them. My home was one of them. For a moment I regretted getting late to go back home.

'It must be from one of the houses.' I told myself without reasoning too much and started walking again though the fear was still in my head. I walked a little faster now, almost running. That's when I heard the laughter again and this time it was louder. It was that of a woman and it was hysterical as if she was mocking me.

I remembered then that my cousin had offered to accompany me halfway down the road around the paddy field but I had refused saying that I love and trust my village to be scared to walk home alone at night!

'What if some *yakshi* catches you!' He had teased me.

'It will catch you too then.' I shot back immediately, laughing.

My grandmother who is now long dead had always entertained us when we were kids, with ghost stories especially that of the '*yakshi*' or a female vampire who feeds on men's blood. Being a man myself, the thought did not escape me now as I hurried; my heart beat picking up pace.

A sudden movement on my left distracted my already disturbed mind. Through the corner of my eye I believe I saw a dark figure standing some distance away. And then the sound of someone running unusually fast through the paddy fields –

the soft splish- splash of water absolutely evident! That's when I started running for my life! I do not know why I ran. Just that I knew with all my being that I had to get away from here! Even though I wanted to run as fast as I could, I felt that my legs weren't able to move as fast as I wanted them too and they couldn't take up the speed my mind wanted.

It was like my mind and body were disconnected by fear. The inevitable happened – I slipped and fell –face down on the muddy path. My torch fell off my hand and into some hole nearby. It was pitch dark now. I wanted to scream. I lay there in fear unable to move, wishing someone came and rescued me. That's when the smell engulfed me.

The smell of the *pala* or the Indian devil tree. I remembered my grandmother's words

'The *yakshi* loves the *pala*. She even lives on the *pala* tree and smells of it. The smell intoxicates her victim as she slowly entices him towards her to drink his blood.'

The smell grew stronger and I felt intoxicated. I knew my end was near and for a moment I resigned to my fate and my unnatural death. I felt something like soft footsteps approach me.

Silence.

Something cold touched my neck. It was a woman's finger!

That's when I started screaming. I have no idea of how long I screamed. In between somewhere, I heard footsteps and noise. I felt a rush of cold air and something swishing past me. I did not stop screaming.

I heard people talking and a man's voice asking me to calm down. Strong arms pulled me up and I was looking into the face of a man, the torch he carried projected ghostly beams on his face. There were two other men with him.

I screamed again and someone asked me again to calm down.

But I was not back in my senses. I couldn't believe these were humans in front of me. I screamed again this time trying to break myself free. That is when one of the guys slapped me right across my face. That calmed me down. They gave me a moment and then asked me why I was screaming. I found myself babbling. I wasn't able to talk. The man asked me to calm down. Then I told him what had happened, my voice shaking.

They walked me home. All the way back home, I was in a daze while the men supported me. Once we reached my house, the men informed my concerned mother and elder brother about how they had found me lying in the middle of the road screaming.

I walked into my room tired and still in shock. My worried mother whispered if I was fine. I said a yes to her but I wasn't fine – not in the least and I wanted to be alone.

'Why was he screaming?' I heard my brother asking the men.

'Do you know Kamala and her daughter Shanti?' I heard one of the men ask my mother and brother. There were three of them; I later recognized them when I was in the sanity of my home. One of them was Madhavan – the only son of a very influential landlord in my village. The other two guys were Madhavan's friends Narendran and Padmanabhan who were from pretty decent families themselves. They were older to me, my brother's age and were quite well known in our village mostly because of Madhavan's father. It was Madhavan who had asked that question. The other two were quiet. From my room, I could hear my mother murmur something but it wasn't audible.

'The first time they realized something was wrong with Shanti was when they found her standing with a knife at her brothers bed while he slept. He woke up on time and was able to run away before she could do something. The doctors who examined her had advised her mother to put her in an institution, which the family did not agree to. Instead they kept her locked up in the house, in a room!' Madhavan said in his strong voice.

I heard my brother ask him the significance of this piece of information.

'Because when we found your son screaming on the road, she was standing over him looking at him. She had a knife in her hand with which she could have hurt him. He is lucky we came on time. The moment she saw us, she ran into the darkness. She was too quick for us.'

They had my full attention now. I felt numb. The same time I felt a miserable laughter cracking up inside me. I tried to control it. I know about Shanti. I have seen her a few times before the so-called house arrest she was in right now. She was one of the most beautiful women I had laid my eyes on and I also knew about how there were many men vying for her attention that is until news started making rounds about her deteriorating mental state.

I could hear my mother weeping and thanking God that I was safe. My brother murmuring something too, something probably on the same note. The men sat chatting with my brother and mother for few more minutes before they left.

The next day we came to know that Shanti was found hanging by her sari, half naked from the branch of a tree close to the paddy field.

I remember not being able to breathe. I also remember feeling very sad. Who could have done this to her? Or if she did it to herself? And when did this happen?

That night my brother came back from work to tell us about a rumor that Shanti was dead for more than a night and there is a rumor that she was murdered.

The moment I heard that I started giggling, my mind going crazy. My mother and brother looked at me surprised.

'What's so funny?' My brother asked.

'Nothing...just that I remember smelling the *Pala* and thinking a *Yakshi* was around me that night'

'So you weren't screaming that night because you thought Shanti was going to hurt you?' My brother asked sarcastically.

I saw my mother's face turn pale. 'A woman who dies an unnatural death will turn into a *yakshi* ...this is what is believed.' She said lost in her thoughts.

My brother was shaking his head in disbelief at the crap he thought my mother was saying. He dismissed what I said and continued

'This is a rumor that she was dead for more than a night. We all know this is nonsense since those men saw her standing over you just yesterday and they were quite sure about it. What's wrong with you both?' And turning to me, 'When did you start believing in all these *yakshis* and ghosts?'

'What if... Madhavan and his friends did something to her and just cooked up this whole story.' I asked. I did not mean to ask it. It just fell out of my mouth like someone else was saying it.

'Be careful of what you talk about him, *mone.*[2] They are very powerful people.' My mother admonished me, a look of fear on her face.

My brother had a smirk on his face. 'Why were you screaming then that night?' He asked me.

I had no answer and I dare not utter another word. He will laugh at me if I swore and told him again that I felt an

2 *'mone' is a Malayalam term used with affection to call your son. Like 'beta' in Hindi*

unnatural presence around me. He will mock me if I told him that I had felt something cold swish past me when the men came looking and that I felt a woman's finger on my neck! What about that deathly laughter I heard? I could feel fear creeping slowly up my spine thinking about it.

I had no idea whether I was right or whether Madhavan and his friends were right. Were they lying or was this all just a figment of my imagination – imagination of a disturbed mind? How did Shanti die then?

I had a dream a week after that. In that I saw three men. I saw a woman. The woman was mentally not well. The men had always eyed the woman because of her beauty. She had run away from home and fallen into the trap of these lewd men. I saw them smother the women to death after they sated their carnal pleasures with her. Waited for the right time to get rid of the body. They found a man screaming in the middle of a muddy path on a moonless night. They cooked up a story and hung the dead woman from a tree.

I woke up in a sweat.

Story started spreading about how I saw Shanti's ghost. Another story that made the rounds was about how Madhavan and his friends rescued me from Shanti who was trying to hurt me and that I saw her minutes before she died.

My relatives came to see me not out of concern but to get their earful about my experience as they gulped down their tea. I did not talk to them. My mother did in her tearful way. After a while she started getting irritated too. Who I did not expect to show at my doorstep, was the police.

It was a casual interrogation. They asked me various questions like did I see Shanti that day? Did Madhavan and his friends really help me that day like he had claimed to the police already?

I told them that there was indeed a woman and I had a feeling she might hurt me but I wasn't sure if it was Shanti. I even confirmed that Madhavan and his friends did help me reach home that day. There was so much more I wanted to say but I did not know how to say.

'It's better you go back.' My mother told me one day way before my vacation was over. 'These people here will cook up many stories. They have no other job. They might even end up calling you mad, possessed or even worse, they might link you in some way to her death. Its better you go back.'

The night before I was supposed to leave town I woke up with another nightmare. I saw a pale woman standing at my bedroom window. She had dark cascading hair, thick and black like a night without stars. Her beauty was not that of a human, but of a supernatural being. She had the *pala* flowers on her hair and she smiled at me – the smell of the *Pala* engulfed my senses, my whole being. I woke up like a dead from a deep slumber feeling my lungs gasp back its life air. I shuddered. I couldn't go back to sleep that night.

Its only when I reached back to Dubai that I finally had my sanity back. The nightmare however kept visiting me once in a while.

As years passed, the more I thought about it, I was convinced that there was more to the story, which I couldn't prove. A little voice somewhere inside told me it was an unnatural experience. I do not know till date. The police had closed the case confirming it as suicide. The stories slowly died away. The only loss here was for Kamala and her family who left the village shortly after.

It's been 30 years now since that incident. I never met Madhavan or his friends after that however their stories never failed to reach my ears.

Madhavan died an unnatural death, drowning in the family pond. He had gone as usual for his evening bath and never returned. His family went looking for him when he had failed to return and found him dead. His eyes had a look of horror in them when he was pulled out of the water as per rumors. What's even more shocking was the fact he was a very good swimmer – his death still remains a mystery.

Narendran,I heard after hearing about Madhavan's untimely demise went into total shock and stopped talking to anyone. He became a total recluse not socializing much with anyone after that. He spent most of his days smoking and drinking. He had once commented to a cousin of his that he feels he couldn't take the weight of guilt that tore into his soul anymore. When the cousin had asked him what was he feeling guilty about, he hadn't answered him.

His wife found him hanging from their bedroom ceiling fan one day. He left a one-line note:

I am sorry for everything.

The last one Padmanabhan is the only one surviving of the three friends. His daughter had an unhappy marriage where her husband almost beat her to death when she had found him with another woman. She was bought back home, a ghost of her former self – the poor woman was broken not just physically but even mentally. When her husband divorced her and she came to know that he was getting married to the woman she found him with, she had taken her life on the day of his marriage.

Padmanabhan takes care of her son now. The once healthy man is now reduced to mere skin and bones, unhappy, broke and bitter.

Last year when I was back in Kerala driving my car, I passed by the same paddy fields and thought about the three guys and their fates. I then wondered why had Madhavan not taken me home that night in his car. There were proper roads leading to my house too. His family had owned not one but two cars during those times and he had his car with him that day. I heard him say that to my mother when he hurried back saying that he left it on the side of the road hearing my screams. Instead he chose to walk with me all the way towards my home. They could have easily dumped me in the car and drove me home. Why did he not do it? Was there something in the car that he and his friends did not want anyone to see?

That laughter. Was it my imagination?

That cold swishing feeling? Was that also my imagination?

If the men saw Shanti standing over me, why did they ask me the reason for me screaming instead of asking me if she had tried hurting me?

Were they really able to see her clearly that night with a knife?

This and many other questions remain unanswered even today.

I then brush it off as usual until I see a pale face again in my dreams on one of those rare nights, teasing me and laughing at me until I beg her to leave me alone.

With time, she left me.

What The Eyes See

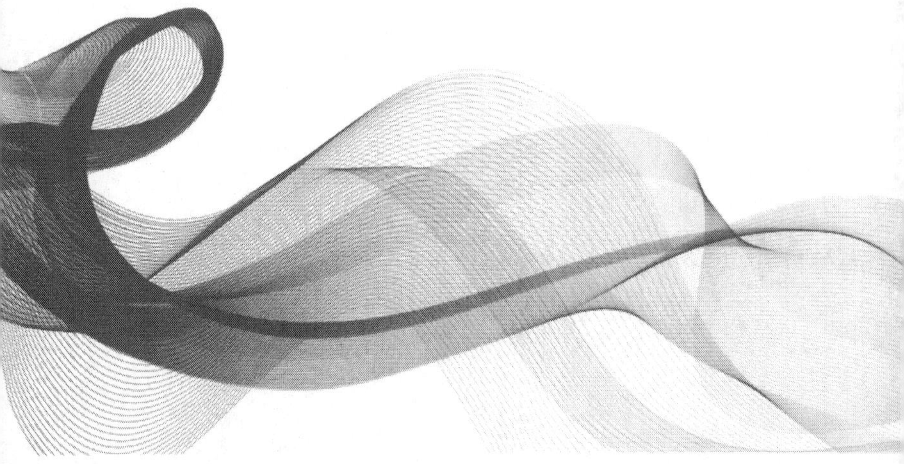

Amna stared onto the blank page on her laptop.

She realized she was in a state of procrastination and emptiness. She couldn't bring herself to write anything. That she was trying to write a book was a secret she kept to herself. Neither her parents nor her sister would support her if they come to know about this. She knew she had a lot of stories in her mind, her imaginations always ran wild (that both her parents and her sister agreed) and hence she had recently decided to put them all together on paper.

Its been 6 months since she lost her job and since then she is shut up alone in her flat (her father's flat to be precise) trying to land a new job. When things did not go her way and she got not a single interview call, she decided to do some freelance work, which came very occasionally, and so now she decided to try a new career path- writing.

Right now sitting in front of the blank page, Amna felt hungry. She was trying to be on a diet because her weight as usual was tipping to the heavier side. In fact she was trying for the last couple of weeks to no avail and right now she was so hungry she felt she could eat a dinosaur.

She opened the fridge to find some leftover rice and the chicken curry she bought over from her sister's house two days back. Her stomach growled at the sight of food and she raised her eyebrows in disdain, not very pleased with her stomach's reaction.

While the food was in the microwave, she poured herself some lemon juice–the ones you get readymade in the grocery store and tasted its bitter sweetness. It was refreshing indeed and she was in the throes of taking another gulp of it when she heard the microwave making weird noises.

When a minute later it exploded, she spat the juice and ran out of the kitchen while thinking if something had hit her face or if it was just a feeling.

Later, when she slowly went back to her kitchen to see what had happened, there was smoke and the microwave was on fire. She stood there watching it not able to comprehend what just happened

'Ma'am, a microwave cannot explode like that.' The security officer was talking to Amna a few minutes later and she wondered if it was a statement or a question.

'But it did.' She said looking dumbfounded. 'You can see it for yourself and the food is burnt!'

'Yeah but....' The security officer seemed confused.

'What? I put it out with a fire extinguisher and had I not done it...' Amna made an exasperated sigh.

The man shook his head. He looked at Amna. A 20 something girl with disheveled hair; big glasses and a dumb look on her face. She seems genuine about what she said, however, he wasn't the least interested to explore this further. Maybe the crazed lady did something. He did not like her – something about her made him feel uneasy.

'I will be in touch with you ma'am, but please be careful.' He assured her as he left the flat.

Amna stood there looking at his back as he walked towards the lift and disappeared inside it later.

She closed her door to go back to the kitchen.

Now I will have to buy a new microwave! Dad won't be happy to hear about this!

The flat she was currently staying in was her dad's. He used to initially rent it out but for the past one year its been without a tenant. That's when Amna stepped in and asked to take it up on rent for a year -the catch being she would pay the rent after she gets a full-time job. It took a lot of convincing and promises of taking care of everything from her side before he had accepted it and now this...

The food was gone and all that she had wished for was some hot rice and chicken curry. She wished it so bad that she could feel her tummy ache. She rushed to get her mobile to call her mother. Maybe she can drive to her parent's house and have some fresh home-cooked food! She could already smell and feel it inside her mouth.

It was when she was dialing that the smell of food struck her. The heavenly smell of freshly cooked chicken curry. She realized that her mind was playing tricks on her but the smell was too strong for it to be some sort of hallucination.

She decided then maybe the smell is from the next flat; her neighbors must be cooking, however, she had never smelt anything cooking before in the few months she had been there. She stopped dialing her mother and held her forehead in irritation.

This is just not good.

The smell grew stronger and tantalizing and she started to have a headache. She followed the smell and reached her dining table. Its there on the table that she found the meal.

In her plate was steaming cooked rice with the chicken curry she loved. Amna's mouth fell open.

This is not right. This can't be happening.

She looked around her nervously, also under the table and went to her bedroom, bathroom, kitchen and also the balcony to check if someone was there. She then called out for her sister. It is her sister for sure, she told herself. But... how can she slip in and leave the food and go unnoticed. Why would she even do that in the first place? Amna slowly touched the rice. She withdrew her hand back like she was burnt. The food was real. She wasn't hallucinating. She was unsure about eating it though. What if it was poisoned?

She swallowed her saliva (as much as she was suspicious, she wanted to put a spoonful of rice and chicken into her mouth). She slowly went back to her phone. She called up her sister Meera. A strong matured voice answered on the other side of the phone.

'Hey! Thanks for the food.' Amna tried to sound casual but there was silence at the other end.

'What food?' Meera replied at last sounding confused.

'The rice and the curry...you somehow...you know what you left here for me.' She felt stupid saying it

She heard Meera give a sarcastic guffaw.

'Is this some kind of a joke which I'm not understanding? Because if it is, I don't have time for it 'coz am at work and AM BUSY! Remember some of us still have a full-time job!' She was back to sounding serious again.

Even though that last sentence was intended to hurt her, Amna chose to ignore it. She heard someone shouting in the background at Meera's end.

'Who is that?'

'Ok, got to go.' Meera disconnected the phone – CLICK!

How rude!

It was a known fact, which was never said aloud to her by her parents or sister – that she was a loser. When she was a child, most of the kids used to ignore her. She was the child who was always lost in her thoughts. She was quite happy in her world of make-believe and magic. She found it very difficult to make friends because she was shy and underconfident. She was so soft in her speech that most times people had to ask her to repeat what she was saying. With time, Amna learned to speak a little louder.

When she became a teenager, she was ignored by guys too. She knew she was average looking but would lie down at night thinking and dreaming about going on a date with the guy she had a crush on. This made her very happy.

She was average in her studies too and hence did not win hearts in that department either. After graduation, she found it difficult to land her first job as an accountant. She was in that job for 5 years after which they laid her off.

Her sister, on the other hand did better than her when it came to everything- she had lots of friends, a steady boyfriend and right now worked as a marketing manager for one of the leading retail firms in the country.

Amna sighed as she turned and looked at the plate on the table again. It was still there. She slowly took the plate with the food on it and moved with it slowly to the kitchen like she was carrying some nuclear waste and dumped it in the dustbin before settling for a cup of pralines ice-cream that she found in her fridge. She gulped it down hungrily and felt satisfied immensely. She fell asleep after that.

When she woke up, it was around four in the afternoon. A sort of weariness set in and she looked around her wishing she were in her parent's home. This whole idea of staying independently, doing freelance work and looking for a full-time job was not feeling all that great. Her money was running out and to top it all, on evenings like these, she was reminded of Akshay and their breakup.

The average looking girl had indeed managed to get into a relationship with a good-looking guy. His name was Akshay. The first time she had met him was at college where he was her senior. She remembers seeing him the first time and thinking about how good-looking he was. They never spoke to each other though in college.

It was after graduation and in the 5th year of her job that she met Akshay again. This time in the lobby of her office building. She was surprised and happy to see that he recognized her though he did not remember her name (*she was very sure he did not even know it to remember).*

He told her that his office had shifted to the same building where she worked. They kept running into each other in the lobby, in the car park and later at restaurants nearby. There were times she would look forward to bumping into him and would sometimes intentionally wait in the lobby around the time she felt he would make an appearance. She had even started giving more attention to her looks – wearing better clothes and even taking the time to put some makeup on. Then one day, he took her number saying they should have lunch together someday. They did not have lunch but he started sending her forwards and messages on whatsapp which she started returning too. Forwards later turned to chats, first it was just good mornings, then lunch invitations along with his colleagues and later just the two of them. The chats grew longer and later extended till goodnights.

'I like talking to you Amna. You are a good listener.' Akshay had once mentioned to her.

Before she knew, she was falling deeply in love with this charming guy. She loved everything about him – his smile, his voice, the way he said certain words, all the PJ's he cracked – everything about him was endearing for Amna.

When she came to know that he was just out of a relationship with his girlfriend of 3 years- she was elated but not cautious. When she lost her job due to a mistake from her end and left the building crying, he had met her in the car park and tried to calm her down. She had hugged him then and told him that she loves him. She thought he had hesitated at first but then even he hugged her back, 'Hey, I love you too Amna.' That was how their relationship started. She was on cloud nine in the months following. He made her feel like she was the best thing in the world – her confidence grew by leaps and bounds.

She remembers thinking about how her batch mates would react when they came to know about her relationship with Akshay (one of the most good looking guys in college) – she was planning on breaking the news to them through her Facebook status update when they would plan to get married. She remembers Meera telling her that it must just be a time pass for him or even worse a rebound relationship. But Amna chose to ignore it. She even went to the extent of calling Meera jealous and Meera had asked her to go to hell. And to hell, she went when things started falling apart with Akshay after about 4 months. At first, he kept ignoring her calls and messages and kept making excuses for not meeting her to do with his pressure at work.

What she did not know was that his ex was back in his life– after 6 months of staying apart. Apparently, they had just taken a break and it wasn't a break-up! It was on her birthday when he did not even bother to wish her that she started getting that funny feeling from the pit of her stomach. She called him several times till she drove up to his apartment. She did not have to even come out of her car. He was with Maya (his ex who was not his ex anymore) at the entrance of his apartment kissing her goodnight and sending her off in her car. She remembers seeing her picture in his apartment earlier when she had visited him. She looked much prettier in person. Amna remembers feeling as if a hot rod was pushed down her throat.

Later when she was screaming at him like a mad person at his apartment without listening to his excuses, he had threatened to call the security if she did not behave herself. It was like someone had poured steaming hot water on her face hearing him say that. When she started crying, he had got irritated with even that.

'Now don't try to make me feel more guilty Amna! Please...please don't spoil your day. It's your birthday. Please leave.' He had tried telling her politely but when he saw she wasn't budging, he threatened to leave the house if she did not. She slowly got out and he closed the door behind her.

That was it. She never met him after that though she tried calling him a couple of times. The first time she called him, she was drunk. She had purposely got drunk to forget the mind numbing pain she was going through of being cheated upon. He had been soft with her and asked her to forget him.

'For me, its always been Maya all along. It took me time to realize it. Please try to be happy for me Amna.' He had told her. She would have slapped him hard if he was in front of her. She had cried hard while he had stayed on the phone with her for sometime before disconnecting. The second time she called was after a week but this time he did not answer. She kept calling him until a woman answered the phone. It was Maya.

'Why don't you leave him alone? Did he not tell you he doesn't love you?!' Maya had shouted at her. Amna wasn't ready for it and had disconnected the call, her heart thudding crazy.

So does that mean she knows about me and my relationship with him?

She had cried herself to sleep that night too. For some reason she couldn't bring herself to accept that Akshay was an a**hole and instead she blamed herself, her weight and her joblessness for the same. Slowly the crying ceased and her heart filled up with a wave of anger towards him and mostly towards Maya. It's been 2 months since the incident and she was still reeling under its effect.

Amna wondered if she knew all along that he was just using her? Had she purposely let him play along to no better reason she could think of- had she somewhere along the way wished for him to truly, irrevocably fall in love with her? Was she foolish or just too adventurous? Was she suicidal when it came to love?

Back to the present, Amna got up groggily from her bed to fix a cup of tea. Half a day was gone and wasted doing nothing and she felt bad about the same. It was when she was fixing her tea, she remembered about the rice and curry she found on the dining table. What was that all about? She went to her dustbin and opened it gingerly. The white rice with the curry did not lie scattered in the bin, as she had left it. It was missing! She took a step back involuntarily and almost got her little finger burnt when she looked to her left and saw the microwave oven the way it was before it had caught fire. It sat there on the counter without a scratch on it and she felt like it looked at her as if it *knew* she was shocked. Her sudden movement had her almost backing and slamming into her pot of tea she had put on the oven and thus the burnt finger.

She sucked the finger as she kept her gaze on the microwave. A funny feeling came over her. A mix of apprehension and horror. She wanted to laugh out loud at what she saw, at the same time she wondered if she was hallucinating. She walked towards the microwave and looked around it. She dared not touch it.

Something told her she shouldn't.

She sucked her burnt finger again as her tea boiled over, her gaze fixed on that damn microwave. Suddenly she turned, switched off the oven and ran out of her house grabbing her bag on the way. She struggled to lock the door as the keys kept slipping off her fingers. She decided to calm down and counted to 5 before bending down to take the keys.

When you get up, the door will be open and there will be a worn-out figure of a dead woman standing there staring right at you

She shushed her thoughts as she slowly got up, half looking up and half looking down.

The door was still closed. She heaved a sigh of relief and calmly locked the door. She was thinking too much and it was time to get her shit together.

She half walked and half-ran towards the elevator, in between looking behind her. She got into the elevator.

I am a very rational person. I only imagine things for entertainment or while I am writing those stories I show no -one. But what if the elevator stops halfway and inside I am trapped with a figure?

She stepped out of the elevator nervously and took the stairs. She was going crazy and she knew it.

Once down, she walked towards the security room. The guard sat at his table happily chatting away to maybe a girlfriend, she assumed. He had that look on his face.

On seeing her, he said something seriously on the phone and hung up.

'Yes ma'am?' He got up and walked towards her.

She fumbled with her key and looked at him carefully, thinking as many times as she could, how to ask him the question.

'Thank you for coming up when I called you but did you find...I mean feel the microwave was burnt?'

He looked at her for a moment, a bit confused.

'Yes...I mean that's what you told us and that that's why the fire alarm went off, isn't it?' He asked cautiously.

She nodded her head nervously.

'You think... it looked ok? I mean I don't have to buy a new one...do I?'

He shrugged his shoulders. 'Ma'am, that's up to you. His phone buzzed again and he looked at it and then back at her.

He must be thinking I am crazy.

'Ok, got to go.' She smiled at him nervously as she left him standing and walked out towards her car.

Once inside the car she composed herself before dialing her sister again. She did not pick up. She dialed again and the phone came switched off. She thought of dialing her mother and then decided against it. She cannot tell her a word of what happened to her today to have her preaching religion and whatnot to her. Amna started the car and drove on, aimless at first before she decided to go to her sister's place.

'What are you doing here AMNA?! You know I can't entertain personal visits!' Meera almost hissed at her.

Amna regretted being there already. Her sister was never a person to be disturbed at work! What a workaholic.

'Hey...I want to talk to you about something that happened today. It's urgent. That's why!' She told her.

'You will have to wait for an hour more until I am off work, that's it!' Meera told Amna and walked inside leaving Amna shocked. She thought of walking out in anger but she waited. She waited for a complete hour and a half before she saw Meera walking out, all smiles and in an animated conversation with her colleague.

She was surprised to see Amna waiting for her.

'You did not leave?' She asked her. Amna shook her head and she could feel hot tears spring up in her eyes. She felt unwanted and humiliated.

'Oh, I am so sorry. I was so immersed in my work that I...' Meera saw that Amna was not looking good at all. She looked like she could breakdown at any moment.

'Come let's go to my place.' Meera hugged her. Big sister mode was back on and the bitch had taken a back seat for now.

2

'You know your imagination runs wild, don't you Amna? I'm hundred percent sure you were just thinking this all up!' Meera gave her an incredulous look.

They were at Meera's flat and Meera found it hard to wrap her head around Amna's microwave and chicken curry story.

Amna did not utter a word. She sat there on Meera's couch, staring at the wall.

'You imagine too much, Amna. I don't know whether to laugh at this or to scold you or to...Wait, are you doing this to just get attention?'

'Support me! Can you support me for once?' Amna whispered.

'All of this is just...getting the best of me. I am scared if I am losing it.'

Meera cooled down then and shook her head. She walked towards Amna and hugged her.

'Nothing like this has happened before. I have NEVER come to you before claiming that something happened the way it happened today and it felt so real that I am going crazy now thinking what the heck happened.'

'Maybe ....we should see a doc.' said Meera rubbing Amna's shoulder. She looked concerned now.

'That's what I am scared of! I don't want to be like grandma!' Amna's voice broke.

There was silence after that. Neither of them uttered a word as both of them delved on their memories of their grandma who they affectionately used to address as Nanuma

Nanuma was a loving and caring human being. She loved

her kids and her grandkids. All including her husband who considered her the harbinger of good luck into his life adored her.

Nanuma like every human being had her problems. She used to have those 'days' when she was not herself. She started to 'see' things after her first delivery when she gave birth to a stillborn son. She was silent for two days not even shedding a tear. A week after that, it started with her seeing her stillborn son in his crib. At first they considered her rantings as something coming from an emotionally distraught mother grieving for her son but later when she refused to come out of the room or tried snapping at or trying to hurt anyone who entered the room which she did in fear of the safety of her son, they had to restrain a screaming Nanuma to her bed and lock her inside. The screaming's faded after sometime into the night.

'She had screamed like a woman possessed.' Amna remembered her great-grandmother telling her mother.

The story continues that Nanuma, the next day, was back to normal. She did not have any recollection of the night before and was shocked to find herself tied to the bed. She went on with her daily duties of a responsible bahu of the house as the family watched her, with everyone apprehensive of what to expect next.

For years later nothing of similar nature happened though her in-laws and her husband used to find her talking to herself once in a while or staring into the wall. It was after her husband and Amna's grandfather's death that she started having episodes again.

She would see her dead husband, her parents and her unborn child. She would go moody, angry and even snap at anyone or everyone who ever tried to talk to her then. She would be like that for a day after which she was back to being the normal and loving grandmother they all knew.

Nanuma's episodes were often discussed in a hushed manner within her family and relatives. When Amna grew up, she saw it happen couple of times when they stayed with Nanuma during the summer holidays. It was scary – the change of demeanor of her loving Nanuma into this weird lady who goes stiff and starts talking to herself and later being taken into a room and being locked up for a day. They never showed her to a doctor. Never. That was what Nanuma's husband, Amna's grandfather, requested.

What will people say? Once you show a doctor, its like we are stamping her to be a mad person.

From what little Amna researched on the internet, she wondered if her grandmother had paranoid schizophrenia.

She wondered if things would have been different for Nanuma had she been treated by a doctor. This is a mental disease and mental diseases are to be treated.

Later when Amna left Meera's house, she was still pensive. She wondered if this is all just her imagination or hallucination. Was she sick like her grandmother? That's the last thing now that she wanted in her already miserable life. She wondered how would Akshay have reacted had she told him about today's incidents. Maybe he would have thought she was crazy or maybe he would have tried to understand it all. She hated the fact that she was still thinking about what he would think.

He is a lying cheat and not the person you thought he was.

From what news she got of him last, he was engaged to be married to that....good for nothing female who kept changing her mind about him. She heard they were getting married in another month's time.

That thought made her sad and she started crying.

He had not even bothered to say a sorry to her for what he did to her.

Maybe she needed closure. Maybe a word or two from him. A sorry or maybe 'I did a big mistake leaving you ... and am back now.' She could see him telling her that in her vivid imagination. He was in her apartment, on her couch sitting next to her and she felt peace with that thought. She missed him. His presence. How she wished she could just talk to him and hear his comforting voice. He had been an oasis of color in her otherwise mundane life. He had been like a trophy she thought she had in her hands but which turned to be just an illusion. Or maybe he still loved her and because he was too good to say no to his ex when she came back to his life, he was still sticking to her.... now why did she not think of this before? Without even thinking twice, Amna now started driving to Akshay's apartment.

She parked her vehicle outside his building from where she could see his balcony. The door was open but she did not see anyone. She knew she won't be able to enter the building and hence she stayed there at her spot waiting to see if he would come out. She stayed there for an hour before she saw someone come out. It was Akshay. He was out for a smoke. Her heart leaped with joy at seeing him. All her worries were gone for a moment as she saw him standing there. But it was short-lived. Maya was out after a few minutes too and was standing beside him. They said something and laughed and Amna watched as Akshay hugged Maya and planted a peck on her cheek -she could feel the insides of her heart burn. How much she hated her! She did not wait longer and drove off trying to fight tears.

She drove aimlessly for a while again lost in her thoughts and thinking about Akshay before she headed back home. Once she reached her building, she passed by the security guard. He did not see her. He was back on his phone. She passed by him quickly. She did not want to face him now and see that judgmental look on his face.

The elevator ride was peaceful unlike what she had had earlier that day but she was not at all prepared for what she saw next.

Akshay stood at her door. She slowed down on seeing him unable to believe her eyes.

I am hallucinating. I really am sick.

He smiled unsure as she approached her door and him. She ignored him as she searched for her keys in her bag. The darkness of being mentally sick suddenly sucked out the remaining light out of her face.

'Amna, you look like you seen a ghost.' He hesitated. She looked at him now confused. Maybe this is how it was – it looks all too real.

'I know you are shocked to see me here but I knew you were at my building...I saw you in fact.' He said and touched her hand. It felt real. He was real. She was out of her reverie as she felt more unsure now than before and dazed. She went back to searching for her keys and now she wondered nervously about his intention on being here as her hand felt the coldness of the key tucked away among her numerous junk in the bag. He was looking at her. She could feel it. She could feel her legs melt – she wondered if he was there to ask her to stop spying on him.

He waited patiently while she opened the door and then she turned to him.

'What do you want?' She asked softly standing at the door, her eyes cast down.

'Amna, can I come inside? I need to talk to you.' The softness in his voice wanted to make her cry.

'For what? Aren't you getting married in a month? Does she know you are here?' She asked him. He did not reply to that and turned back to walk.

She sighed as she went to the kitchen to get some water and to calm herself down.

What am I doing? What is happening? Does he really want to talk to me?

She looked at the microwave. It sat there without a scratch on its surface-unharmed and untouched. She felt the nauseating feeling of fear recalling all that had transpired during the day. She went back to find Akshay and saw him standing near the elevator. When she called out to him, he did not hesitate for a moment. He walked back towards her, a sort of happiness etched out in his face.

She invited him inside and when he made himself comfortable on the couch, she took a seat opposite him. They sat there looking at each other for some time, neither one uttering a word.

When he finally opened his mouth to say something, she cut him off, 'You were not right in doing this to me, Akshay.'

Akshay sat there not saying a word. Then slowly he began, 'I am sorry Amna. I am really sorry.' He said softly and he sounded like he meant it.

It was like an ocean had unleashed as she let out her tears. She cried for everything – for the morning, the frustration she had with her sister, at seeing him again and hating herself for feeling so peaceful and even allowing him to get inside her house. She hated herself for that and yet she was feeling so happy it happened.

Akshay moved and sat next to her.

'When Maya came back, I couldn't tell her a no. It took me time to realize that. I always knew it in the back of my mind and I guess I just kept denying it.'

Amna looked at him wiping her tears away.

'I always felt empty and today when I saw you, I realized something that I always knew- that I missed you.'

'Amna, I did a big mistake leaving you and am back now.' He said to her, tenderness in his eyes.

Amna stopped crying and looked at him. Even though her heart was threatening to break with all the emotions, there was now a new feeling of discomfort.

I have seen this somewhere, haven't I? He was sitting here on my couch and holding my hand and uttering these same words. I pictured this today in my mind, didn't I?

She was suddenly alert now as she looked at him. She did not know whether to believe what sat in front of her or to be scared.

'I mean it.' He said and she knew he was sincere about it. 'The moment Maya left home, I decided to come over and meet you Amna. I am sure now. I will tell her that I can't be with her anymore.' Amna looked at him, still not sure what to say.

But am not sure Akshay. I am not sure if you are real or not. I am not sure if this is again one of my hallucinations or...or something else.

She wasn't sure because another thought ate away at the back of her head. She had been writing that novel in the morning and was imagining in all her vividity that microwave oven catching fire – one of those random lazy thoughts and imaginations when she read that it can't explode. And why did it bother her? Because it happened just before her eyes just the way she had imagined it.

She knew it all the while and yet she blocked it right in her head. And the food that appeared, she had wished hard for that too with all her heart, hadn't she? That too had appeared in front of her eyes and come true. Now Akshay was right in front of her just the way she wanted him telling her that he was wrong and was back.

It was a sudden sense of exhilaration that ran through her as she ran the thought over and over in her head for all the possibilities. Akshay looked at her confused at her reactions.

But is he the real thing or some mirage?

She excused herself saying she needed to get a grasp over herself and went to the bathroom. Once inside, she sat on the closet contemplating. She was sure when she gets out, he won't be there.

Am I having some sort of a superpower?

Na...can't be. She can hear Meera sneer at her. 'Not again, Amna. Not again! Go and see a doctor please!' She could hear Meera in her head.

She slowly opened the bathroom door and peeped outside. She saw Akshay on the couch still busy on his phone.

He is still there.

She closed the door and dialed a number on her phone. The line on the other end was ringing and someone answered it

'Are you kidding me?' Akshay answered on the other end.

'Why are you calling me?' He seemed shocked.

'I am...I am... just called to know how are you?'

Akshay started laughing. 'You got to be kidding me. You can talk to me once you are out. Is this some kind of a joke?'

She disconnected the call.

He is the real thing.

She opened the door to find him standing there with a grin. Without waiting for her to say anything, he took her in his arms and kissed her hard. She forgot everything then and closed her eyes.

He is indeed the real thing. He is here and he loves me.

'You have to leave Akshay,' She told him once she was able to breathe normal again. There were many other things she wanted to tell him, but she couldn't. She did not want him to leave but she wanted to think and understand all that was happening now.

'Are... you sure?' He looked disappointed and a bit taken back.

'Very sure. I need time to think. I will call you.' She opened the door for him. She walked with him outside and accompanied him to his car. On her way back she saw the security guard looking at her and ignored him.

Once back at the room, she fixed herself a cup of coffee and made herself comfortable on the couch before brining her thoughts to the events of the day.

Is it possible? Is it possible she can make things happen just by wishing for them in all their vividity? She looked around in the room and wondered.

'I wish for a bowl of hot soup.' She said out loud.

Nothing happened. She tried her luck again many times wishing for various things. Nothing. Does it stop at three wishes like Aladdin and the magic lamp?

Has it stopped working? Am I just crazy even to think this?

Maybe you need to wish it with all your heart?

Even if it was true and she could manifest what she wanted, it did not stay that way for long. It seemed to have some sort of a timeframe after which it ceases to exist.

She felt sadness at the thought of it. She looked at the phone lying on the ground. It's been an hour since Akshay left home. 2 hours since she wished to see him at her doorstep.

He was here and wanted to be back with her. That shone a light on her cloudy heart – a light she so wanted to follow. She picked up her phone to call Akshay. He did not answer immediately and when he did he sounded like he was in the bathroom.

'Akshay, I wanted to let you know...' She hesitated. Is she doing the right thing? Will he leave her again?

'I wanted to let you know that I want to be...'

She heard a female voice in the background ask 'Is it her again?' as he disconnected the call and she felt her cheeks flush. She called back again but this time there was no answer.

What the hell is she doing talking to an engaged guy. She is being such an idiot! He had left her to be in the arms of the wretch who called out to him. He would never leave her. She should have known better. He was and always will be a lying cheat!

She threw the phone in anger.

I wont let that guy get into my head again. Maybe he is bored and looking for a time pass. He knew he could use me for the same because he KNOWS I still have feelings for him.

She felt bitterness and anger seeping into her. She felt humiliated.

She wanted to give him a piece of her mind. She took the phone and dialed again. The phone stopped ringing. She dialed the number again. This time the call got disconnected. She called again. This time the phone was answered by Maya, 'I can't believe you have the guts to call again, you whore!'

Amna sat there listening to her without being able to reply. It was like the cat caught her tongue.

'How could you call back again, you...' She couldn't complete her sentence because Akshay had taken the phone from her.

'Amna, what the hell is wrong with you and why do you keep calling me again and again!?' He sounded angry now.

'You were the one who came to see me today!! You wanted

to be back with me! And you ask me why am I calling you?!' Amna who had found her voice now, shouted back

'You are a crazy woman! I was at my home the whole time! Get yourself treated you...' He hung up sounding incredulous.

She threw the phone again in anger. She wanted to scream. She was hyperventilating.

How could she do this to herself? How could he do this to her?! She had her respect intact until he came waltzing in today and she let herself go and now he is back with her doing what...disconnecting her calls and calling her CRAZY! How dare he do this to her! And that wretch of a woman, how dare she call her a whore? Does she even know the meaning of it? She suddenly remembered her standing in that balcony and laughing with Akshay – how she wished it was she instead of Maya standing there with him. How she wished Maya was never there in the picture. How much she wished Maya was dead! How much pleasure it would be to see that happen? How much pleasure it would be to see HIM in pain.... Oh how she wished.

She suddenly realized the darkness of her thoughts and felt guilty about it but the thought was there in the back of her mind teasing and tantalizing her just a little bit. Before she knew she was in her car driving again to his flat

How could he do this to me...she was overcome with fatigue. All her energy was invested in hate, sadness and the emotions overflowing from that day.

Coz your wish has timed out, you silly...a little voice inside her said flatly but she paid it no heed. She was parked at the same spot she always had. The balcony was clearly visible from here. It had become her sweet-sour spot. The lights were still on which meant they hadn't slept yet. She was too tired to think of anything more. She just wanted to lie down somewhere and sleep it all away. Slowly, before she realized, she fell into a deep slumber.

She had bad dreams. She was in a room with Maya. Maya kept calling her a *whore...whore ...whore* and Amna slapped her before she wringed her neck. She could feel her hate pulsing through her hands and her blood boil as she felt the life trickle out of Maya slowly...

She woke up with a start to find herself in her apartment. It was dark inside her room. The curtains were drawn. She must have over-slept. She suddenly remembered driving to Akshay's place. She got up suddenly feeling very dizzy. She wondered how she ended up back in the apartment. She had no recollection of anything... it scared her. Her phone was switched off – the charge must have drained out. She took it to her bedroom and connected it to the charger near her bedside with the little light from the street outside that shone into her room. Her hands felt dirty and she switched on the bedside lamp to see what was on her hands.

She couldn't recognize the animal-like wail she heard that came from her mouth while she fell on the floor in an agonizing pain. Her eyes had darkness setting in and she found that she couldn't breathe. She scrambled on the ground and forced herself to breathe trying to swallow the air in big gulps for her to help breathe. When she finally regained her breath, she got up nervously and ran to the bathroom and turned on the tap.

She washed her bloodied hands under it. Blood that did not seem to leave her skin. It wasn't her blood she knew it.

She knew whose blood it was.

The phone rang now. She did not answer it

It was my wish. I wished it with all my heart, didn't I? Maybe it will go away like how others happened. Oh God how I wish this is just that!

She simply couldn't recollect anything. It was as if she had blacked out...

The phone rang again – persistent.

Feeling tired and nervous, she answered the call. She did not even look who called. She was too dazed for that.

'You filthy bitch! I can't imagine you did this!! Don't think you can escape. The police are coming for you and in case they don't get you, I will get my hands on you and when I do, you are done!!' It was Akshay sounding like he has never sounded before – screaming at her, yelling at the top of his voice. Her wonderful, loving Akshay.

'I was right in leaving you!! You are crazy with a capital C...you... You were a big mistake! Oh God, how could I even do this to myself! Thank God I came on time else you would have killed her you.... Psychopath!'

Wait. She isn't dead?

'How could you!!! How could you...' He was sobbing now. Someone behind him was trying to calm him down ...

She heard a click on the other side of the phone. Aghast at what could have happened, she took the phone and banged it repeatedly on the wall, screaming her lungs out all this while.

I have to call Meera! Something is wrong with me. Something is wrong with me. Hallucinations or superpower, I am not normal.

I have to reach Meera else I will go crazy

I have to reach Meera before the police gets here.

I have to reach Meera because I tried to kill someone.

She looked at her phone now trying to calm down. It wasn't working. She tried switching it on and off a million times, nothing. She heard a police siren in the distance and stopped in between. She put the phone down, got out of her apartment and ran downstairs. She took the stairs.

The security guard was fast asleep on his chair. His phone lay on the desk in front of him. She peeped in and took his phone. Thankfully it wasn't locked. She dialed Meera's number.

The police siren was getting nearer now.

The ring seemed to go on forever. Meera must be asleep but she HAS to answer now.

Please, oh please answer the call, Meera!! At least now...at least today.

3

A few minutes later, the police found Amna cuddled up in her bedroom like a fetus with the security guard's mobile in her hand. She was shivering. When they tried to pull her up, she started screaming and apologizing. It took two or three of them to pull her up and get her hands cuffed.

'No...I did not do this. I don't even recollect...it's just like a mirage...it will go in a while...you just have to wait... please let me explain.' She just went on ranting.

'Please ...please, please...listen to me.' She kept requesting.

When they pulled her out of her room, she started sobbing. Through her tears she wished it would all go away.

But nothing happened.

It will not happen because this was all just your hallucination. This was all just a story you saw in your mind, wasn't it? You had no super power, you are just sick in your head! Sick, sick, sick, in your head!!

They pushed her into the elevator to take her down the building while tried to struggle herself off. They held her tight and pushed her down. Once the elevator reached down, they dragged her up and pushed her outside. Outside the building, people were slowly gathering who had come to see why the police was there.

The security guard stood there, with pity in his eyes.

How will you ever face your parents again? How will you ever face your sister again!! Before, you were just a normal loser but now you are a murderer!!

She closed her eyes tight and wished it all away crying.

4

The ting on the microwave had Amna open her eyes again. The rice and chicken curry were ready. Her stomach growled. She kept the lemon juice back in the fridge and took the food out of the microwave. The aroma was so good.

She took the food to her table and settled down, pouring herself a glass of water. She took a spoonful of rice and curry in her mouth savoring it to its fullest.

That was a pretty good story you imagined up Amna. A story about wishing so hard that things start happening...even the bad ones.

She smiled at herself and her idea and shook her head as she took another spoonful of rice–Now if only she could put this story she saw in her head onto paper with ease. If only!

Behind her unknown to her, the laptop turned on and words started appearing on her word document.

Karma

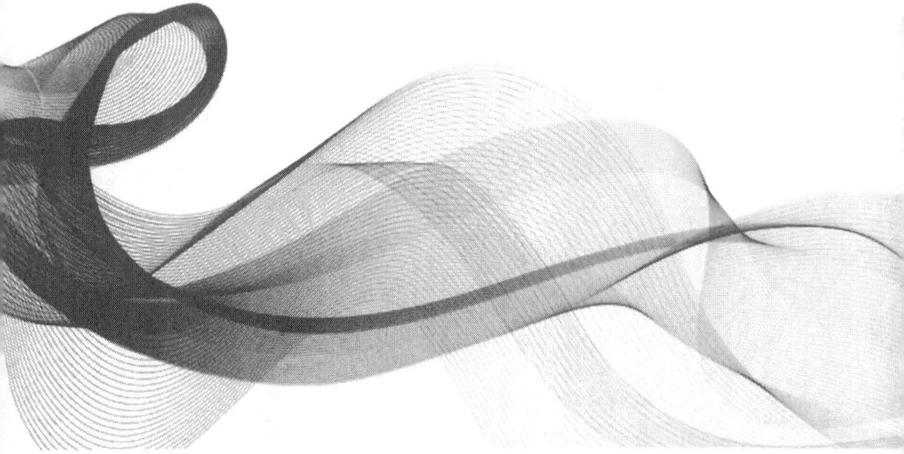

When Jai Dixit died, not many people cried.

As a matter of fact, the only person present at his funeral was his father. The doctor pronounced him dead Sunday morning and by Monday morning he was cremated according to traditional Hindu rituals; his ashes scattered in the Arabian Sea as per his wish.

Maybe that's why he wasn't doomed to wander the lands he was supposed to leave behind after death because Jai's death wasn't a natural death. He was murdered.

That he was dead and that he was no more a '*he*' was very evident to him as he saw from afar, his body being burnt on the pyre.

His father was the only one present from his family, his eyes wet. Jai could feel his pain. It was like he experienced the pain rather than feel it and it ran through the form that he was in right now. But at the same time he felt free. He felt like a balloon whose air was let off or like a kite that had suddenly found its freedom or even better like a bird that was caged for a long time and was now set free. Caged by the weight of the damned heart, the logic of the brain, the feelings that every organ in his body weighed upon him. The light awaited him and into the light he flew.

He reached a vast expanse of light which was the gateway to the main light that glowed like the sun that attracted him like a moth to the fire, so much so that his very being wanted to melt with it. However, he was stopped from going further.

He knew who was waiting for him there.

'*You failed again.*' The words he expected to hear.

A white being walked into his line of vision as Jai's form stood there in exhilaration of the being. It was as if a sort of happiness now burst through him.

One by one he remembered. It was like a curtain was lifted. He saw it all in a kaleidoscope of colors beyond what as a human he could have comprehended -everything from how he was born to this moment.

'The human emotion of greed and lust. That is what your topic was. I hope you remember?' The being asked him.

Jai or Jai's form understood what was being referred to and so did the figure in front of him.

'Its time for you to rest so I request you to go to the resting place. There is a lot of negative energy in you. Its time for you to extinguish that all from your form to be pure again...then we will discuss how to take this forward.'

2

The next time they met, the being asked

'Do you remember how you died?'

'Yes.' Replied Jai.

His wife's brother had murdered him.

'And you very well know what made him do that?' Asked the being

He saw that clearly too. He saw it all.

He was born as the only child into a family of teachers. His grandfather was the headmaster of a local school and his parents were well-respected teachers. His mother had conceived him after two miscarriages and hence when he was born, he was treated like a little prince; his parents mostly giving into his whims and fancies as much as they can.

He grew up to be a handsome young man. To add to his good looks, he was a smooth talker too. Girls were waiting to be serenaded by him and Jai used and misused the fact to his advantage. The only girl he had stayed away from was Anu. She was the daughter of his dad's best friend and also his neighbor. For some reason, around her, he always behaved his best and never tried to mislead her even though she was attractive in her own way and had her share of men trying to woo her. She was a very cheerful and charming girl and he always enjoyed her company.

It was when they were teenagers, Jai remembered a friend asking him, 'Why are you not trying your luck on Anu, *yaar*? She is pretty. She is someone I would like to marry some day. What a girl!'

'She is not dumb and moreover she sees through all the shit I talk. She can never think of being with a person like me and neither do I want her to.' Jai had replied back as they smoked their cigarettes stealthily in the night without being caught.

'She is my friend and not some girl I would just like to take to bed. I do not want to destroy our relationship.' He continued staring into the night.

But the next day he had walked up to her and taken her by the hand to a secluded place near their house saying he wants to have a word with her.

'What is it Jai? What is happening?' Anu had asked him concerned.

'Anu, I think I am in love with you.' He said looking straight into her eyes.

She looked at him for a while before saying, 'I have to go now. I will talk to you later.' He couldn't understand the tone of her voice. It sounded very mechanical. She was about to leave when he caught her by her hand. When she slapped him hard across his face, he was caught by surprise because he never expected her to do that. She walked away leaving him stunned. He did not sleep that night nor the night after that. He couldn't take her out of his mind. He felt angry towards her but he also felt guilty. Maybe he was too hard on her. Maybe he shouldn't have taken her by surprise. He did not even understand why he did that in the first place. A week passed since Anu spoke to him. She neither acknowledged him nor looked his way. She avoided him like a pest. When he started missing her that's when he realized that he had feelings for her, which were more than just friendship. When he got his admission confirmed to one of the leading universities in Mumbai, he packed his bag and decided to leave his memories and feelings for Anu behind.

'I can get better girls than you Anu. You can screw off.' He told himself as he sat on the train and waved to his parents who had come to see him off. For some reason he half expected her to turn up at the station.

'You really liked Anu but she wasn't the type who could be won over by smooth talks and good looks and hence you never tried. But then you had the time of your life at the University, didn't you?' The being looked at him.

He definitely did. He met a lot of girls inside and outside his college. He had numerous affairs and he never felt guilty about anything he did. Slowly he grew arrogant. The only thing he realized he needed now to feel complete was money – so much of it. He was tired of being from a middle class family and yearned to make it to the next level.

That is when he met Preethi.

It was at a telephone booth that he first saw her. She studied in a different college than his and was there to accompany a friend who came to make a call. He was having a heated argument with his father with regards to money

'What do you do with the money that we send you, Jai!' His father was admonishing him. Jai remembered getting very irritated and even thinking for the nth time about why he wasn't born into a wealthier family.

'I am cooking the money and having it for dinner!' He snapped.

'How dare you talk to your father like that? My hard earned money is not for you to waste on the sluts you meet there!'

That did it. Jai had slammed the phone and walked out. Preethi stood there and seeing Jai had suppressed a smile. She had heard the last sentence he had retorted into the phone. She had not escaped his notice either. She wasn't beautiful but cute in a very endearing way.

His friend who waited for him outside asked him if everything was ok which he dismissed as the usual shit with his father and started walking away.

'You saw that girl there? Preethi?' His friend asked.

'The one with the cute face?'

'Yes.'

His friend had then informed him about how she is from a rich family. Her family owned one of the leading retail businesses in the country and she was the only daughter.

Though he had dismissed his friend, after two days, he had purposely planted himself in front of her college after digging out all details about her nonchalantly from his friend and elsewhere. He was in the last year of college and he knew exactly what he wanted to do once he graduated. He needed money to start something on his own and he knew he could not get the same from his father.

When Preethi walked out, he had stood there smiling at her and he had seen how shy she was. There was no looking back after that. Within no time, he had her dangling around his little finger. The girl was madly in love with him. *'Why do you think your wife's brother put an end to you?' The beings voice cut through the fog of memories that he saw.*

Once he graduated, he had slowly started putting the idea of marriage into Preethi's head. Within no time he learnt that Preethi was the soft spot of her father and brother and that they would do anything to keep her happy. She had completely fallen for his charms and had fought with her father and brother, even threatened suicide if she was not allowed to marry 'the man of her dreams'. Finally they relented.

'You did the act of marriage which is sacred to many humans and was sacred for Preethi too, for the sake of money. You promised a life long commitment to her which you knew very well you weren't planning to keep.' The being did not sound very happy.

He had married Preethi for money. He wanted her money to start out his own business

He was even threatened by Preethi's brother Prakash before marriage. 'I have enquired a lot about you and heard a lot of stale stories about you. But from what Preethi says, you seem to be in love with her. Are you ready to mend your ways else all I can say is, stay away from my sister!'

Jai convinced Prakash that he has never been so much in love ever before the way he is with Preethi and that in fact he never knew what love was until he met her. Such was his convincing power which he often used to his advantage that the very seasoned Prakash fell for it.

'You could have backed out then.' The being conveyed to him. 'But you didn't.'

He didn't. He considered himself too smart and charming to work out his way from anything that a human life threw at him. He was very confident he could get his cake and eat it too

-without anyone knowing about it.

Jai's parents being from a middle class family and being teachers by profession had always tried to instill some moral into him, which never worked. However they did not realize the mess he was getting himself into either. They just saw a Jai who was in love and getting married to a girl who had hopelessly fallen in love with him. They just knew that the girl was from a very rich family though they kept hearing rumors about her brother and father being notorious gangsters apart from owning a thriving retail business. Nonetheless, they loved Preethi.

After marriage Jai started a business with the help of Preethi's father. He gradually felt that Jai was a very capable and smart guy which had helped to loosen his defense towards him.

The father was also ready to do anything to ensure that the daughter lived a good life. She was born with a golden spoon and her father was ready to ensure that the golden spoon remained intact. He even gifted the newly weds a posh bungalow to which they moved in immediately after the wedding.

From his side, Jai tried to be faithful to his wife. *Tried.* After all, the money that he had now or was assured he will have, was not something he wanted to lose so the once in a while escapades he had- he ensured were never found out.

'That is when you fell for lust.' The beings voice had disapproval written over it.

Yes, that is when he had met Esha. She was nothing short of enticing. He hadn't met a woman like her ever in his life. Everyone was eager to fall for his charms, his good looks and ready to jump into bed with him but not her. She reminded him of Anu but a very beautiful Anu. The first time he saw Esha, she was one among the girls waiting for the interview for the post of a marketing manager in his company. He couldn't take his eyes off her. He remembered thinking about her in his bed. Running his hand along her curves and tasting her lips. It didn't take him long to decide who he was appointing. Esha it was.

Things however did not go the way he planned.

'She was very tough to crack and you ended up wanting her more.' The being continued.

She was a beauty with brains. She successfully helped his business reach out to people. She was also bursting with ideas and strategies that amazed him. Many a times Jai would wonder why he had not thought of something like that in the first place.

His lust for her however never died. The first time he touched her without her approval, she had put her resignation letter. He apologized to her and almost begged her though he was fuming with anger inside. He did not want the news to spread and reach his in-laws and above all he did not want to lose a resource like her. She had forgiven him and come back to work after thinking about it for a week. A week that had him walk around like a bunch of open nerves. It taxed him to no end that he almost fell sick until he heard it back from her.

'At least then you could have changed but...no. She was a 'challenge' for you. A prize you just wanted to win at any cost.' The being was sarcastic

It took sometime but eventually Jai and Esha grew close. He never stopped trying and try he did now in his own subtle way without infuriating her again.

With time Esha grew very fond of Jai and she finally gave him what he wanted all along. He couldn't get enough of her then. The bed was on fire with her. She was like a female equivalent of him and they would spend hours making love in places where they wouldn't be found. He was now an expert in not being found out.

'Do you think it was just lust or love?' The being asked Jai. Jai did not answer.

Together Jai and Esha were a successful team. His business was flourishing and Preethi now adored him all the more. His in-laws started seeing him in a new light of respect. He was a very happy human being. He had everything. Money, a non-fussy wife and a good lay on the side. What did not come though was a child. Preethi had miscarried twice.

'They backed out at the last moment...' The being just shrugged his shoulders. He was talking about those souls who had at the last moment backed out from the option of being born as Jai's child.

'I did not push them either, seeing the way you were faring.' The being raised his eyebrows in sarcasm.

Jai soon realized that Esha wasn't what he thought her to be. She was laying a trap for him too. All the acting coy, all the resistance she had shown to his charms and to his attention were merely well thought out actions to make him fall for her.

'I was ready to jump into bed with you the first day I met you,' he remembered her telling him after a night of heated passion in her flat. It had caught Jai by surprise.

Seeing the look on his face, she continued, 'Had I shown my interest in you initially, you would have not been THIS interested in me'

'Really?' Joked Jai. She had hugged him then and looked into his eyes before asking the next question.

'Don't you think we should get married? I am so fed up of all this hide and seek.' Though the question caught him off-guard, Jai had managed to bring up a smile. 'I was thinking the same...' and kissed her.

He had no intentions of marrying her.

Jai had dismissed it as a very casual question Esha asked and even forgotten all about it until she asked about it again another day when they were alone in the meeting room. This time she looked a tad more serious than she did when she mentioned it first to him.

'Jai, you must understand that I love you. I cannot go on like this anymore. Can you try and take a decision about this?' She had told him suddenly after other members in the meeting had left.

'What are you talking about Esha?' Jai was least expecting what she said next. 'Lets be together Jai. Lets get married. Don't you want to?' She looked weary

'Of course I want to. Just that...just that I need time. You know about my in-laws, don't you? I need to think of a way I can get rid of Preethi without hurting their feelings.' He was quick to answer though inside him, he started feeling nervous about this whole thing. It did not show on his face though. Not at all. Esha had nodded in agreement then.

But it did not stop there. The question about marriage kept cropping up on several occasions with increasing frequency and Jai kept assuring her that he is working on it.

'It's about the right time, baby.' He kept telling her.

Eventually Esha grew frustrated. She realized that Jai was taking her for a ride and one day walked into his office and threatened to expose their affair. Jai calmed her but had broken down in front of her. With tears in his eyes he told Esha about how he tried telling Preethi many times but couldn't.

'Crocodile tears. You were so good at this, weren't you?' The being looked at him like a teacher looks at a student, a bit amused but at the same time not happy with what he did.

'I don't want to lose you, Esha. Please know that. I want to be with you. Preethi is so lifeless and so... I can't stay with her any longer. Maybe we should elope?' He had looked at Esha and she had looked confused.

'Why are you quite?' Jai had prodded.

'Jai, take your time but not more than a month.' She had said finally with a resolve.

'What you did after that is what started paving way towards your death warrant.' The being shook his head again.

Jai knew by then that he had to corner her and make her weak else she would keep haunting him with the marriage proposition. He was in no way planning on marrying Esha. She was just the woman he could never be comfortable living with under the same roof.

Esha had come to work one day to realize she was terminated with immediate effect. The reason given out to her was unethical conduct.

A raging Esha had walked into Jai's room demanding an explanation.

'There is no explanation Esha. I came to know you were slandering the company name as well as mine by making up stories and spreading the same. Plus I have got a hint as to you giving out company secrets to competition. I can't believe you did this! I helped you grow and in turn you do this to me!' He had shouted at her.

'I ...I don't understand. These are false accusations! There is some mistake!' She had said back angry but weary, a bit confused again.

'Do you want me to queue up the witnesses before you?' He had challenged her. She looked at him incredulous.

He had then walked up to her and taken her by the shoulder and looked into her eyes 'I know there might be some mistake but I can't do anything when there is evidence presented to me...please try to understand.'

There was pain in her eyes as he let go of her and said, 'Let's meet up later. I think you should leave now'

The being was shaking his head again. 'You watch a lot of movies, don't you? That move, the looking into the eyes...what was happening?'

A day after that incident Prakash had confronted Jai at his office. He had held him up the wall and demanded an explanation on the rumors he heard as to why he had fired Esha.

'She was spreading ...stories about me and her and about the company ...bad stories. She was a blood sucking pest and I came to know she is been leaking company secrets too to our competition.' He had said half choked. Prakash had put him down then

'I am a man too Jai and I know every man has his own physical needs. Whatever said and done if Preethi gets upset then you are done, remember that she still trusts you and we don't want to see that trust broken.' Prakash warned him.

That day he had gone home and taken Preethi shopping. He got her a pair of beautiful diamond earrings.

The being chuckled.

Esha called him again after two days.

'How come you haven't even contacted me after that?!' She had screamed at him.

'Esha! Do you know Prakash came to me asking about us?' She went silent. 'He threatened to kill me before he left.' He continued in a dramatic tone.

'I need to meet you Jai' She had said then.

'It's not possible now!' Jai said flatly.

'Fine, then wait for the shock that's coming your way!' She had said coolly. Jai had become alert then. He agreed then to meet her out in a public place -a coffee shop.

He had reached there early and had ordered his coffee at the counter when he saw a familiar looking face standing there at the counter.

'Anu?' He had exclaimed looking at her.

Anu looked at him surprised. Her straight face had then cracked into a big grin. She looked beautiful and happy.

'Jai! Its such a surprise to see you here!' She had told him then. There was genuine happiness in her eyes. She came and hugged him.

'Its been so long! How have you been? You just... disappeared.' She was grinning.

He felt something shift inside him then. It was like a ray of sunlight just touched his life. She always had that effect on him, her aura was so colorful.

'What are you doing here?' He asked her as they moved out from the counter to a corner in the coffee shop.

'Oh, am just here visiting a friend. I am leaving today.' She said.

'What about you? How is your wife? I knew you got married from your parents.'

'Oh, she is fine. She is good. I am doing good too...started my own business and am doing pretty good.'

'Good for you.' She had said cheerfully.

He wanted to ask her more about her life. Was she married? Was she dating someone? He wanted to spend more time with her when he heard Esha behind him.

'Hi Jai.'

He turned to look at her face and felt the darkness close on him again. What was he doing with his life?

'I think you got company, Jai? Let me leave then.' Anu

said then.

'Wait, let me give you my card. Give me a call when you are free.' He had given her his card and she had left. He felt heaviness set in his heart as he watched her leave.

'New girlfriend?' Esha had asked him sarcastically.

'Come, let's talk.' He had told her ignoring her question and controlling his anger. He did not like anyone talking in that tone about Anu.

She sat at the table and sulked and he hated himself now as he looked at her for getting into this affair with her. What the hell is he doing?

'Who is that new slut?' She finally had asked about Anu. That is what was bothering her.

'She is not a slut. She is an old friend.' Jai had hissed at her then.

'Did you tell your wife, Jai?' Esha ignored his answer and moved herself forward to the table, her eyes locked on him.

'No, I did not and I don't intend to either'

'And may I ask WHY?' She wasn't angry nor was she upset.

'I never told you I love you Esha. You know that very well. We were just having a good time together. You and me. You knew very well I was married. It was you who came up with this thing about marriage. I thought you were different. You had everything. Marriage is asking for too much. You are just like the other women I know. What a shame!' He had been sarcastic. He did not try to hide it. He was done with her. He did not feel an ounce of attraction for her anymore. He wanted someone new now.

He saw her fuming

'Well, then wait till your wife knows about us.' She had

threatened.

'No one is going to believe you Esha. I have taken care of that!' He had told her arrogantly.

She had smirked at him.

'You really think so? Think again. You keep telling how smart I am. Don't you think I am smart enough to film one of our passionate times together?'

She suddenly pulled out her phone from her bag and browsed through it and showed a video clip to him. She had indeed filmed one of their passionate nights together. The volume was turned on high and her moaning's could be heard inside the coffee shop. Many people turned to look at them.

He looked at her in horror.

'Stop it now.' He hissed at her, his face turning red.

'If you decide to pass me off as one of your filthy flings, this video will be going to your wife and your in-laws.' There was a look of triumph in her eyes as she shut the video and the moaning's ceased.

'If you send it to them, they will kill us both. Don't think you will be spared!' He almost shouted at her.

'I don't mind dying if it means you go down with me.' There was a blankness in her eyes and for a moment he wondered if she was crazy.

His rage returned as she gave him three weeks time to get rid of his wife and then walked away leaving him fuming.

'Maybe for a moment then you regretted your actions however you still never tried correcting them, did you?' The being looked at Jai with disapproval.

No, he did not. The next day evening while he was at home having dinner with Preethi she told him cheerfully about how she met Esha at the mall.

'The poor thing, Jai. I am sure whatever rumors were

there was just made up. She told me she has a boyfriend who is very powerful and he did this to her! She is so broken. She has invited me to her house next week.' Preethi had said while chewing on her food.

A surge of horror took over him.

'Why do you have to go and see her, Preethi?'

'It's ok, Jai. This way people will also realize that there is nothing between you guys.' She had said naively and he felt a lump in his throat. That was it. Esha was going too far.

When he called her, she told him that she was ensuring that he knew she wasn't joking at all about her threat and disconnected the call.

He realized then that he would soon be ruined. He will lose everything he had worked for till now. What's worse, his wife's family might beat him and leave him for dead or worse, murder him!

Even if they didn't he couldn't imagine spending his life again tied to one woman and that also a woman he has no interest in anymore. And even if he were married to her, she would never be easy to fool unlike his wife who was so much in love with him that she was blind to everything he did.

Get rid of her. A voice in him had whispered.

He couldn't believe he even thought that way.

'Neither could I. You know very well Jai that the other voice of reason was me who asked you not to do it?' The being asked.

Jai looked at him and nodded. What about the one that asked him to get rid of her?

'That was also me.' The being looked guilty. Jai looked at him shocked.

'What? You were being tested Jai and you had to chose. You had to choose the right option but you did not do it. I was just

doing my job.' The being said flatly.

'I was always there giving you both the options and wishing for you to chose the right one but you disappointed me big time.'

Jai plotted Esha's murder for several days. Its amazing the way the human mind would calmly assure itself that what it was doing was the right thing. She was an unnecessary burden right now. A parasite. Had she behaved, she would still have been working in his company right now and who knows he might have made sure she lived a pretty good life along with a promotion or two. But she had to bring marriage in between and spoil it all and now blackmail him.

The more he planned it, the surer he was he could carry it off. Meanwhile, there were a whole lot of complaints about his increasing absence at work.

He also started getting pretty irate at home. While earlier he was soft spoken with his wife, now he was snapping at her. Everything she did was a big mistake to him. In his mind he cursed her and himself for getting trapped in this marriage. Later when he was out of the haze of anger and cooled down, he would apologize to her for his scathing words. He had taken to drinking at work and at home.

'Hiding guilt and problems under intoxication is a coward's way out.' The being said.

Three weeks had passed and time was up.

'Nothing monumental to talk about here, right? You were still firm about going forward with the act you had decided upon.' Jai heard pity and sarcasm in the being's voice

The day he was supposed to get back to Esha, he got into a bawl with one of his managers when a joke he said in jest about Esha went wrong. Jai almost beat him to a pulp.

The being gave a big sigh

He was taken home where Preethi was in tears asking him a hundred times what was going wrong and if it was something she did.

He shouted at her and asked her to keep her mouth shut but she wouldn't. The woman was in despair and before he realized, he had given her a tight slap before strutting away to his room to sleep. He was in the depths of intoxication-his only way of escaping reality and everything that was happening to him.

When he woke up, it was nighttime. The house seemed empty. He walked into the living room to find his father-in-law waiting for him. He was seated on their couch. Jai did not expect to see him there and he suddenly felt scared.

'Where is Preethi?' He managed to ask softly.

'Listen to me carefully, Jai. You don't seem to be in the best of your senses.' His father-in-law's voice was as authoritative as the first time he had met him. The man does command respect and Jai stood listening without uttering a single word.

'Preethi is at home now. We took her after she called to tell us about what happened today with you.' He said and Jai shivered a little at that.

'We have taken care of the guy whom you had beaten up. He was ready to go to the police but we have calmed him down. Offered a large sum of money. He took it and is willing to remain silent. But that is not what is of concern here.' He stopped to observe Jai for sometime. He scanned him from head to toe and back up again.

'I realize that you are not on the best of your behavior with Preethi for the past many weeks.' He said softly and Jai opened his mouth to deny the same but his father-in-law had put up his hand to ask him to keep quiet. 'I do not and will not interfere in a man's business with his wife and wasn't planning to either until today she called us and told us what happened. Touching her in any way that causes pain, I will not tolerate and also because for your information, she is pregnant.' He said softly but firmly.

That sentence suddenly had his attention. He was listening more intently now. A sort of sadness took over him.

'At last Jai...your conscience could reach you!' The being told him.

'Be careful with my daughter and remember she can live without you!' His father-in-law told him. It did not sound like a threat but Jai knew it was one given in a very subtle way.

After his father-in-law left, Jai sat down to sort out his thoughts. He decided to call Esha and talk to her. Maybe make a deal with her.

'What do you want? Did you tell her?' Esha did not seem very happy to get his call.

'I want to talk to you. Can I come over?'

There was a pause after which she agreed. She lived alone in a flat in a posh area in Mumbai. Jai had helped her get it during their good times and he used to visit her often, always in some sort of disguise

He took a taxi to a place near her building and then walked all the way. He did not want to take a chance incase things turned nasty. He sported a beard and glasses as he entered her building.

She stayed on the 10th floor of the building and all he could think about was how he could push her off her balcony, a thought that lingered at the back of his mind but which now he was not planning to execute.

When she opened the door, she stood there looking like her old self, just like the time he met her –glowing and beautiful. He had fallen for this and he had not even tried to keep his feelings in check. And here now she stands looking still the same where as he was losing control over himself.

'At last you decided to come?' She mocked him.

He walked inside and was pleasantly taken over by the

warmth of her house, which he had forgotten about. If only she had not brought up marriage!

'I am going to become a father Esha.' He announced to her and he broke down crying. He did not know what made him cry.

Oh quit acting Jai. What are you trying to do? Who are you trying to convince? Don't forget she is very-very smart. He remembers hearing that in his head.

But he wasn't acting, was he? Those tears were real. They were tears of frustration and pent up anger and all that negativity of planning a goddamn murder! Oh God, a murder! He just wanted to go back and lead a normal life and bury his physical urges for sometime

Sometime until everything settles down and you can think of a better way to get rid of her, isn't it? Jai had heard it again.

Jai looked at the being now. 'Like I said I was just doing my job,' he raised his eyebrows at him and shrugged.

Esha had looked confused at his sudden outburst. He took use of the situation.

'I am a very bad person. I want to change and I want to lead a normal life. I am ready to do anything to make it up to you Esha. Just leave me alone. I am going to be a father and you for one know how bad it is for a child to grow up fatherless. You have told me so yourself.'

Esha had grown up fatherless and had to face the taunts and jeers with regards to who her father was since she was a child. That sentence did hit her. Something seemed to shift in her as he looked at her. She was silent for a very long time before she said, 'I just want to let you know Jai that I am leaving India for good. I am shifting to Canada. In between all this madness, I got my PR approved. I was in two minds about leaving this place because of you.'

He looked at her trying to conceal his happiness. She had mentioned to him long back about applying for a Canadian Permanent Residence. He hadn't given much importance to it then.

'I think somewhere along the way, I fell in love with you. I expected the same from you but I guess it was just one way.' She said solemnly.

Jai shook his head.

'I still like you a lot. I still want you to come back and work for me. Together we were a great team. I can still give you a great life. Don't go Esha. Stay back.'

Don't stay back, he said inside his head.

Esha shook her head and now it was her turn to cry.

'I am so sorry! This is so not me...Wait a second.' She went into her bedroom and was gone for a while.

When she came back, she looked more composed and had a USB drive in her hand.

'This is the video I shot.'

She gave it to him

'I don't need this anymore. You can destroy it. I will be gone soon and...let's never meet again. Let's put this all behind us.' She said softly.

Jai got up to hug her however she did not allow the same.

'I am scared I might change my mind, Jai. Please leave!'

Jai hesitated for a while looking at her, maybe even scared that she might change her mind. He then turned and walked out of the flat. He heard her lock the door. Inside, his heart was leaping with joy—joy of having had this easy and joy of getting rid of her at last!

Wasn't it a bit too easy? He heard it in his head.

He went home that day and slept. For the first time in

ages, he had a sound sleep.

The next day morning he got up fresh and decided to go and get Preethi back. He felt light and free. There was a message on his whatsapp. It was from Preethi.

'Where are you?'

He was happy to see it.

'I am coming today to see you and to take you back home.' He replied.

She sent a smiling emoji back.

He got dressed up and went on his way. When he reached the gates of Preethi's house and went inside, he got a call from Esha.

'Where are you?'

'I am at Preethi's house. Just came to get her back.'

'Oh...Just wanted you to know that am on my way to the airport.'

For a moment he was stunned. He wasn't expecting her to leave so early. Maybe after a week. She had not mentioned anything to him the day before.

'I just wanted you to know Jai that the last three weeks I thought a lot about us and our affair and had felt that I wasn't doing the right thing and once I got my Canadian PR, I was hundred percent sure that I should let this go and even destroy the video I made. I had made up my mind about that and had decided to leave without even letting you know. A door of opportunity had opened for me and I was feeling like a very different person that is until you came waltzing in yesterday evening with that big act of yours and I could feel all the rage building up again in me!' She said very calmly

He wasn't prepared for that and for a moment felt lost.

'I am not like all the other women you have slept with. Women like my mother and me fall for men like you and my father and give you our all and you just use us and dispose us like garbage. I know you very well and just because of that I know that you don't have a bone in you that cares for another person. You are the most selfish bastard I have come across in my life and you should be taught a lesson. You think I fell for your tears? I didn't. In fact I planned to send that video by whatsapp to your wife today and I already did. She has already seen it. So Goodbye and good luck!'

She disconnected the call.

No! No! No! She can't be doing this. He could feel the blood draining from his face. His hands and legs felt weak as he tried to call her back but she disconnected his call every time.

When he called the last time, her phone was switched off.

The bitch!!

'You should have known better Jai, don't you think so?' The being looked at him sadly.

'How many chances did you have to mend yourself? You just didn't. I was fed up of giving you chances.'

Jai looked at the being and felt a kind of remorse for the first time he was there in the light.

'What happened next was quite gruesome, wasn't it?' The being asked.

Jai had tried to run away from the house before anyone could see him. But he was too late. The gates were closed and he was dragged by his leg to one of the SUV's by Prakash

'Papa was very soft on you but this even he cannot forgive.' He remembered Prakash telling him, his face red with rage as Jai screamed to let him go, apologizing for all that happened. They had gagged him and taken him to some far away remote place and bludgeoned him to death.

He remembered the horror of it. The pain and treachery

of it–suddenly he was able to feel it all again. Like his human self. How was this possible?

'Just giving you a reminder of the pain you have to go through incase you fail this test again!' The being scolded him.

'Fail the test?' Jai felt surprised.

'Yes. As you very well know, the ultimate aim of every soul is to lessen its karma and purify itself to be one with the light.' The being explained to him.

The light. Yes the very light that shone around them. The very light that attracted him like a bee to a flower. He could see many forms far away walking into the light and disappearing and he could see many coming out from the light and disappearing too.

'You have three options now in front of you.' The being came down to business.

'Option one, pay for your failures by living a life in hell. A birth with only misery and treachery around you until the time you die and come back here. You can be back with the light if you choose after that.'

'Option two, be born as Preethi's child. Pay for your sins with the life you lead and pay back for the treachery you put her through. Once that is done, you can again be one with the light.

And Option three, go back there and do this all over again. You will have no recollection of doing this before. It will be like starting all over again on a white sheet but in a different dimension like.' The being concluded

The being smiled at him and Jai wondered how many times has he done this before.

'Oh, you wouldn't want to know that. It's better that way.' The being told him.

'Before you decide on anything, let me show you how it would have been had you chosen to control your vices.' The being

pointed his finger towards the horizon.

Jai saw it.

He was married to Anu and they had two beautiful children. He felt peace and happiness and love. She loved him as much as he loved her. He had even managed to start his own business, which went on to become one of the leading brands in retail in the country. He along with Anu even did a lot of charity work and opened up orphanages and old age homes giving a lot of help and relief to a lot of people. He went on to die rich, famous and old, wrapped up cozily in his bed. Anu was his ticket to the light.

'How is it possible? She never loved me.' Jai spoke now.

'That's what you thought. You were so caught up with yourself that you had no time to see others' feelings or what others wanted.' Said the being.

When he had opened up about his feelings to Anu, she was unsure about it. Her mind was in a turmoil. She always had very special feelings for Jai but she did not trust him to love her. For him, relationships were just a time pass. She knew about his numerous affairs and did not trust him to consider her any different. When he had told her that he loved her, she just saw it as farce. After slapping him, which she herself was taken aback about, she wished for him to get back to her and to convince her that she was the one for him and it wasn't just a passing affair for him either. But he never did that. Once he saw that she wasn't giving in, he ignored her completely. It broke her heart.

'She was even there at the rail station when you left for your University. But you never saw her! You were just too blind under your ego.' The being said pointedly.

'To add more, she even came looking for you in Mumbai. She missed you a lot and thought of letting you know about her true feelings but that is when she came to know you were getting

married to Preethi! Missed opportunity again Jai.' The being laughed now.

'Let me give you some advice. Try to choose a different option this time if you can.'

Jai looked at the being and made his decision.

When Jai Dixit was born, his parents were quite exhilarated. They always wanted a boy child and today God had answered their prayers. Jai's father took him from the hands of the nurse and kissed his tender face.

'You are going to do us all proud, am sure about that.' He said and kissed him again. The baby snuggled into his arms as he slept.

The Angel Numbers

'The devil is an angel too...'

- Unknown

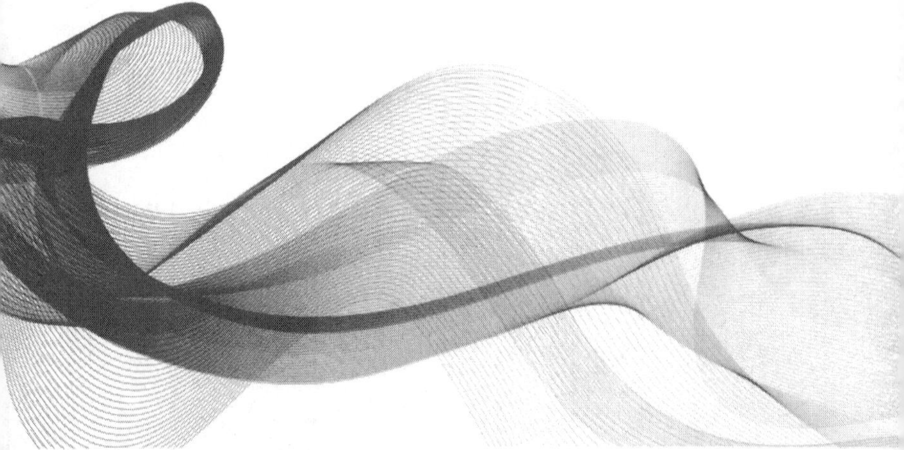

The first time I saw 2:22 on my phone was the start of it all.

I have heard about the angel numbers. The lucky ones who have seen it told me it brings good luck. They even told me it was the angels trying to send messages to mortal beings and hence it was called the angel numbers.

Today the angel number blinked hard and bright on my phone as I looked at it dully. I dismissed it. I dissed anything and everything religious or angelic at the moment. I couldn't stomach the mere mention of anything positive because I was on a joyride into negativity and loathing.

I was asked to leave my current job because I was rude to my reporting manager. I tell you he deserved the cuss words I dished out to him. But that's not what everyone else thought. Not even the ones who supported me behind him and who were unhappy with him.

'He is not a boss...just a bloody ***licker. Just sucking up to the big boss.' We used to discuss during the smoke breaks – self-appointed cigarette breaks. We puffed out not just wafts of smoke but also frustration that left its smell on our shirts as we toddled back in, half the heart left outside evaporating in the hot summer sun. We were a team not just with regards to the work we did but also to a shared dislike of the boss.

But that particular day, when I finally gave the boss a piece of my mind, everything was forgotten. We were no longer cigarette buddies or colleagues who bonded over a common enemy. Suddenly they were on *his* side, giving me the stares, asking me without asking me, *how could you even talk to your boss like that!?* Bloody *** ***es, I tell you. They don't have a spine. Not one of them. They are scared of losing their jobs.

The market is down and finding another job would not be easy and hence they decided to join the opposing team, the enemy team. I feel pity for them.

As for me, I walked out of there once I was asked to leave, not even looking at one of them and not feeling even a morsel of guilt.

You see there is a set of people – friends, relatives and the likes who consider me an arrogant son of a bitch, thankless and ungrateful because I was born into a very well to do family!

My dad apart from having his own little successful business out here also was smart and clever enough (according to the others) to amass a good amount of fortune in the means of property and other investments in India. The fact that he was married to a woman from a wealthy family- my mother, did help him but easily forgotten by everyone.

He has one very lucky son (*I hope you can hear the sarcasm in my tone*) – ME, Nikhil Abraham.

I was born and raised in Dubai. I had a happy childhood- I will not complain about that. My mom was my world. She was also like my good friend. I could tell her anything and everything that happened with friends, teachers or even my school crushes. My dad was busy most of the time. However, when he was around, he ensured he spent time with me and mom, enquiring about school, homework, friends and the likes. It was a safe cocoon I was bred in and I was unaware of the harsh realities of the real world until it was time for me to leave for India to do my graduation.

Two things happened that year. My parents divorced and my childhood crush turned girlfriend dumped me. I was devastated.

My parents informed me about the upcoming divorce 2 weeks before I was leaving to join University in India. I remember them calling me to the living room. They had very strange looks on their faces but I did not even assume for a minute what was coming.

I was shocked to say the least. They tried explaining about how they wanted me to complete my schooling before they decided to part ways but everything they said just flew over my head. They wanted me to complete my schooling? So from when were they having issues and what were the issues? I couldn't believe what they were saying. I even thought they were trying to pull a prank on me until my mother started weeping. For some reason I got very angry then and turned on my dad, 'You were cheating on her, weren't you?' I had accused him. I couldn't get a better explanation for this. As per what I saw and understood, my mother was always at home taking care of me and keeping me happy whereas my dad, his late-night works and his barely being at home started to make a different sense now. A hard slap fell on my face.

'Be careful of what you say.' My mother said visibly upset. My dad was silent and looked upset. I barely spoke to them after that. The week that followed was torture for me even though my parents tried to get me at ease. My mom apologized to me and my dad was very soft with me but I did not want to talk to them- I felt betrayed especially by my mother.

'If you are really sorry, why don't you guys stay together, for me?' I asked her one-day after she tried talking to me.

'We did Nick. All this while we stayed together just for you. We feel this is the right time. We had decided on this when you were a child.' She had said softly then. The only thing she never answers or even my dad for that matter is the reason why they were separating.

I just wanted to get out of there. I felt I did not know my parents anymore. The safe cocoon was falling apart; in fact, it was burning and I wanted to fly away before I burnt myself anymore.

It was during that week that Seema, my girlfriend told me that she cannot 'do this' anymore. She gave no reason, just that she was bored with me! She was flying to India too but a different city to do her University. I don't want to go further on it. I later realized that maybe I was looking for some type of comfort and she was the one who seemed to be around and available. I had been quite heartbroken at that time with the breakup. I felt the whole world was against me however today when I think about it, I am sure that had we still been in a relationship, we would have been suffocated and broken up anyway later on.

Once I left to India for University, I stayed at a hostel. At first I hated it and sulked in my misery and the change of environment. That year was a very long year for me. I felt I couldn't concentrate on my studies. My love for Maths and numbers seemed to have flown out of the window. The ragging which went on for 3 months just added to my misery and unease. I was always singled out by the seniors and made an example of, because they felt I was too grumpy. My professors looked down on me too because of my poor performance in exams – I was never that person and this new side disgusted me.

Six months later, my parents got divorced. I barely spoke to them on the phone or even when they came down to meet me – I wanted them to understand that I was still not out of it. I stayed back in the hostel during holidays when others left to be with their families. By the end of the year, my mom announced that she is getting married to another guy. The shock was back. I did not talk to her for a month. She married some guy called Mathew from Delhi who was based in Dubai. I barely managed to pass my first year of college. A few months later, my dad got married to a divorcee.

It was then I realized that my parents have started

sidelining me. I was just informed about the wedding. They never discussed it with me. They never asked me if I was ok with it (*not that I would have given them a positive answer*). Whether I was upset or not, did not matter to them. It was about their lives now. They had simple court marriages and I did not attend either of them. They did not force me either. Things took a turn after that. Grief was replaced by anger and resentment.

With anger came the will to do better in college. My studies started picking up and so did my relationship with my college mates. I was among the top performing students now. People who looked down on me started seeing me in a different light. Slowly with it came arrogance. I was brutal when it came to ragging – after a few warnings, I stopped it but I kept getting into some trouble or other in college. I was ready to jump into a fight every now and then. The college informed my parents the only reason they weren't throwing me out of college was because I was the college topper. They flew down to see me (to advise me) but I asked them to get lost and told them I will do as I pleased.

The money kept coming in from my dad and mom and was not even accounted for. They thought they could keep me happy with the money but they were wrong. They had lost me.

The visits continued. My mother was careful not to bring her new husband, however not my dad. He brought his new wife, my stepmother, to meet me while I tried my best to not be rude with her though in the end I did exactly that and they had to leave.

By the beginning of the third year of college, I came to know that I was going to have a sibling. My mother was pregnant. By end of the year she had given birth to a boy and named him Nathan. I did not feel anything then. Her phone calls died down for sometime. It was during that year that I came to know by means of a wayward comment from a relative that my mother got married to a guy she was in a relationship with for a long time. I was shattered to learn that but refrained from asking my mother or my father about it. Later when my mother got in touch with me again, I realized that I could never feel the same connection with her, which I had before. Somewhere I felt I was lost.

By the last year of college, I had managed to secure a job in a leading IT firm in India. The cloud had shifted from my life for sometime and I looked forward to joining the firm. It was short-lived. My anger and my attitude worked against me (I don't want to go into that story) and before I realized, I was kicked out. After months of job search and not being able to find something I wanted, I reluctantly agreed to come back to Dubai and join my dad's IT company in Dubai. Things did not go well there either. I had to compete there with my dad's protégé – A guy named Arun, just couple of years older to me and who for some reason had my dad's attention and confidence more than I. What was more irritating, I was put under him, reporting to him. The first few months I tried to be normal and to keep my ego in check but before long, I started resenting him and the fact that he had an upper hand over my dad. During meetings and brainstorming sessions, my opinions or my suggestions mostly used to be swept aside by Arun with my dad totally agreeing with him.

It reached a boiling point one day when Arun told me to get a hang on my attitude and to take things in stride and that's when I gave him a piece of my mind. He stood there, his mouth open, shocked and unable to react to the cuss words dished out to him.

'This is my dad's company, damn it and I don't need to take lessons from you!' I had shouted at him before walking out of the office to calm myself down. That was it. I was called for a meeting after that and asked to apologize or to leave. I chose the latter. And thus I left my last job about which I mentioned in the beginning of this story. Yes, it was my dad's firm but yes, the boss was Arun. When I had walked out of there, I felt a sense of freedom and happiness.

My sense of happiness was short-lived. A week or two went by with lazy mornings, nights out partying and sleeping late into the afternoons. Another two weeks and I started sensing anger towards everyone around me. None of my so-called friends or colleagues bothered to check how I was doing or if I needed any help with getting a job. The only people who did call were my mom and my dad.

'Nick, dad told me about what happened at work. When did you start behaving like this?' My mom asked me sounding concerned.

'How is your new husband and child doing?' I shot back, my voice filled with contempt.

There was deathly silence for a few minutes on the other end that I started counting mentally to see how long she is going to be quite. In a way, I relished the fact that I could shut her up.

'What are your plans now Nick?' She decided to completely ignore my question.

'Nothing that I think you should be concerned about.' I said without a hint of emotion. She did not let that affect her either.

'Nick, why don't you come home? Its been a while you met Nathan.' She said. After coming to Dubai, I had met her and her family once. I felt a pang of jealousy, I must say, when I saw Nathan with my mom. Even though I despised him when I came to know of his birth, I remember seeing him the first time and realizing that I couldn't hate this cute little thing. As for my mother's husband, I did not care and did not talk much with either. 'I don't think I have time...' I said.

'Its Christmas Nick, we all are meeting at my place for

dinner this time. I want you to come please.' She said softly.

'I will try.' I said and till date I don't even know why I said that. Maybe a part of me still wanted to be back on normal terms with my mother. The Christmas dinner was to happen a few days down the lane and to be attended even by my dad and stepmom. This is not the first time they were meeting for dinner. In fact over the years while I was in college the four of them had got into a pretty good relationship with each other – unbelievable.

The only person who seemed to have been left out was me. Out in the cold.

My dad tried to talk to me many times after the incident with Arun but I wasn't ready to listen to him – my message was clear, its either Arun or me.

On the day of the dinner, I arrived late. I wanted to spend as less time as possible with all of them. I realized that other than my parents and their spouses, only my cousin Sid was present along with Nathan. Sid was staying alone in Dubai and was of my age.

The evening was progressing well with me spending time with Nathan and Sid. They were the only people around whom I felt comfortable with. Nathan showed me the nativity scene he had put together with my mom with the angels he collected and baby Jesus. I could again feel the slight tingle of jealousy it created in me. I used to do this with my mom when I was a child.

'I love angels.' Nathan told me cheerfully and I smiled at him, my heart still burning. My stepmom as usual tried to make small talk with me and I as usual remained diplomatic with her. The same went to my step dad too. They were beginning to nauseate me slowly.

It was while dinner was served that all hell broke loose. I later wondered what exactly had me behaving that way? Was it pent up anger? Was it pent up resentment or was it seeing that nativity scene?

My dad who did not bring up the topic of my behavior at office thought that he could finally serve that to the others along with starters.

'Nick, I really think that your behavior was unacceptable.' He said to me in a matter of fact tone. I did not reply to that and purposely sipped on my soup loudly.

It drew a disgusted look from Nathan.

'Arun is a very nice and hardworking guy. I thought you could learn from him and that is why I put you under him!' It was as if he was apologizing for his actions.

I did not reply to that either. I saw my stepmother looking at me with pity in her eyes.

He did not stop there. He went on to discuss about my attitude and my anger problems, my wasted talent and the likes. He said he was concerned about my future if I was to go forward with the same attitude. I could feel that my hand had folded itself into a fist and that I was trying to keep my anger in check.

I decided to ignore him. He stopped in between realizing that I am not listening to him.

'You know what your problem is, Nick? You know that you have money to fall back upon and that is why this arrogance, this lame approach to life. Your mother is very worried about you.' My step dad suddenly said that.

That did it. The soup bowl went shattering on the wall beside me, its contents adorning it. I saw that Nathan had a shocked look on his face.

'I am done here.' I said and got up to leave. I was so fuming with anger that before leaving the table I took the entire bowl of chicken stew and threw it on the floor. Some of it splattered on to my face and on to Nathan's new trousers. He started crying.

'Get a grip over yourself Nick!' My mom's voice was stern but staggered and she was up and near my side in no time.

'Stay away from me...' I shook myself violently off her grip.

'I would have rather you died than seeing you with this man!' I spat at her. 'You gave importance to your relation with this man over your family, over me!' I could feel the vein in my neck pulsing. I saw the color drain from her face.

I walked up to the door and saw the angels and baby Jesus. My anger grew and I kicked them. They all fell down and some of them broke. Nathan was now wailing loudly. My father was beside me now.

'Nick, get a hold over yourself and apologize to your mom. That is not something you say to your mother!' He was controlling his emotions and his anger. His face had turned red. I felt happy seeing that.

'You have no right to tell me what to do. You have NO RIGHT to tell me about how to live my life. Look at you. You couldn't keep the family together. Your wife left you for this guy!' The anger from all those years poured as pure poison into my words.

'Mind your words Nick...' His voice was a whisper.

'You blame me for what is happening in my life? Well I BLAME you and her!! Anything that's happening in my life today, I BLAME you both.' I shouted at my mom and dad.

'Enough!' My dads voice was slightly raised now. 'Its true that we separated and yes it was unfair to you in a way but we have tried our level best to keep you and make you feel comfortable. You are a grown up man now. Own up your life NICK!'

'FUCK YOU' I hissed at him and opened the door to

leave.

When I left, I saw my mother weeping, my step dad trying to console Nathan and the look of contempt on my step mom's face – the bitch. Sid stood with my dad who looked lost and embarrassed. I did not feel any regret. They deserved this.

2

There were phone calls. Sid called followed by my dad and my mom. I did not attend any calls. I was at home trying to get wasted and finished four to five cans of beer.

My mother sent a few whatsapp voice messages telling me that she loved me a lot and she is sorry for any pain she has caused me. I deleted all of them. I been hearing this for a long time.

The phone rang again. It was my dad calling again. I answered it to give him a piece of my mind but saw that the phone had gotten disconnected.

I sighed and looked at the time on the phone.

There it was again. 2:22.

I threw the phone and went to sleep.

I was dreaming. I knew it. There was fire around me. Cities burnt.

I got up with a start to some sort of beep on the phone. I looked at my phone groggily to understand the time. It was 2:22 on the phone. I looked at it for a while, half sleepy, thinking that maybe my phone isn't working. I got up to drink water , my head feeling heavy. It was when I was back in bed that I felt it.

The air in the room was different.

Heavier. I then smelt it- something burning. I panicked wondering if I left something burning on the stove. I jumped out of bed feeling unusually warm. I turned and walked to my window. The curtains were blacked out but I could feel it.

I opened the curtain to see a sight I will never forget. From the 12th floor of my apartment, I saw the block I lived in, the road adjacent to it and away from it until my eyes could reach, the city burned. I took a sudden movement backward out of sheer shock and fell on my bed, my mouth open, my eyes trying to adjust to my surroundings, trying to see if am at the right place. I could feel my heart sitting right in my throat.

Within a while, I was back to my senses and I scrambled out of the room . I ran out of my flat to the corridor to find it empty. *How can it be empty?* I could hear my heart beat – *thud-a-thud, thud-a- thud.* Am I the only one who is awake and seeing this? I knocked on doors to see if someone else is aware of what was happening. Not a single door opened.

'Hellooo', my sound was an echo in the corridor.

'Helloooooo', I called out again in despair. *Was this some sort of an apocalypse!*

Outside, I heard something like a blast and the next minute I was running. What happened ? Is this some sort of a war?

I ran down the stairs one by one, my heart racing. I reached the exit and out I jumped. I was sweating and panting like a dog. The buildings around me were burning so were the cars parked around it. I could hear screams but I couldn't see anyone. The building I stayed for some reason was not burning but I knew that very soon the fire would spread there too. I ran to the security desk and found it empty. I ran outside again through another exit and that's when I had the horror of my life.

There were people alright and they were burning. There were dead bodies all around me. The ones that were screaming were on fire and they were either on the ground struggling with the fire or trying to run away with fire on them. Out until my eyes could reach, I could see fire everywhere. The city was indeed burning. This is war. They dropped some kind of a bomb or something, but who? The screaming...oh the screaming, I have never heard anything like this even in my nightmares.

I thought about my family then. I wondered if they were ok. I could feel tears spring up in my eye and that is when I saw a figure walking lazily towards me. The smoke covered him as he toddled towards me. Around me people were still screaming. I could smell burning flesh and feel the heat of the fire. The smoke threatened to choke me.

'Hey! Are you ok?' I cried out to the figure.

I started coughing as the smoke started getting to me. My vision was slowly dimming due to the smoke.

This person, as he came nearer, I realized had a smile on his face. This crazy person who seemed to be ok as he stood there and looked at me. He wore jeans similar to the one I was wearing with a black t- shirt. His eyes though were very visible through the smoke along with his very crooked smile. His eyes – they stood out like light in the dark. They looked almost yellow.

And that smile...that very creepy smile.

Don't cry little one. I don't like the crying you. Don't become too empathetic towards your family especially that no good mother of yours.'

I was hearing him in my head. I knew it was him. I stood there looking at him as he bore into me with his hypnotizing eyes.

You are perfect the way you are. I am on your side. You are right and they are wrong. They ought to be taught a lesson. Don't change, don't you dare.

I felt scared then standing there. He walked towards me and stopped in between. That look made a scream originate at the end of my gut but which got muffled way before it came out of my throat.

He started laughing. It was a maniac laughing.

I wanted to ask him who he was. Something about him was pure evil.

He laughed again and this time I could feel the heat covering me up. I felt the fire on me and saw it lapping at my feet and before I knew it was upto my neck building its way up to my face. I started screaming. He laughed and laughed.

I woke up in my bed drenched in sweat still screaming. Once I came to my senses I looked around me. Everything seemed normal. I got out of bed and rushed to the window and opened the curtains. It was very quite outside. No buildings were burning nor were there people screaming. It was a nightmare. A nightmare that seemed too real.I couldn't sleep after that. I walked into the kitchen and poured myself a cup of coffee and sat at my balcony sipping on the same until the sun came up. By the time everyone else was awake, I was snoring away to glory.

It was an interview call that woke me up later that day at around 11 am.

It was for a company I always wanted to work with. I don't remember though sending them my CV. The recruiter, a lady asked me a few questions and fixed up a date for the first round of interview with the HR head of the company. I completed the call and unknowingly checked the time on the phone. It was 11:30 am. I heaved a sign of relief. The nightmare and the reality of it were still fresh on my mind. Who was it that I saw in my dream? The phone rang. It was Sid.

'I don't know what got over you yesterday. After you left, everyone was upset. Your dad was very-very silent after that.'

I did not reply to that.

'Can you come over to the café below my office? Lets

chat?'.

I told him I will be there in an hour. If I was my usual self, I would have just disconnected the call and went on with my life but not today. Today I felt something different. Maybe it was the interview call or maybe it was the nightmare. I wasn't sure. In 20 minutes' time, I got dressed and headed to my car in the parking lot. When I started my car and slowly headed on to the main road, I found myself debating on whether I should meet up with Sid after all.

To hell with them all...!

Whatever happened next was too quick for me to even comprehend.

I heard a earth splattering crash as I moved on to the main road. For a moment I was distracted by a ting on my phone.

It showed 2:22. It froze me for a second that I did not see a four wheeler coming from the side in break neck speed.

It was blank after that. A sort of blinding whiteness surrounded me. I could hear voices, sirens, but I was floating most of the time.

Then I could feel an unbearable pain on my left side and below my waist. I wanted to scream but I couldn't. It was so painful that I wanted to cry and somewhere deep inside I feared a figure I might see again. It then went silent and then dark.

When I came to my senses it was like pulling myself out off a pool of cold water. I gasped for air as I got up and my throat hurt. My heartbeat stood still for a moment. When I started breathing again, I looked around me. I was in a very familiar room .I tried to recollect my thoughts and remembered then about the accident. I sat up with a jerk on a bed that felt oddly familiar. I looked around me; my eyes trying to adjust to the surroundings. I realized it was night time and the curtains drawn in front of me allowed faint city lights into the room.

I was supposed to be in a hospital or maybe even dead or was that another crazy nightmare?

I saw a small Donald duck figurine on the side table with a photograph of me when I was about 9 or 8 years old. The sudden realization took me aback. I realized it's my old home where I stayed with my parents.

I got out from the bed and looked around me. This was not possible. I was in my old room. My room where I had spent most of my childhood and my teenage till I left for University. Did they bring me back here for some reason? How long was I gone? How is it that I don't have a single bruise on my body? I looked at the Donald duck trying to understand how it got back there. I had thrown it in the dustbin in anger when I left home.

I slowly opened the door and looked around. An old familiarity greeted me. I even smelt it. My heart felt heavy at this. I tiptoed out. The air-conditioning was on to beat the summer heat as how it always used to be in our house.

I saw a light in the kitchen and slowly walked towards it. I peeped in and saw my mother sit there, her eyes had a far away look and she was in her nightclothes.

There was something else. She also seemed very-very young, the way I remembered her when I was a kid. This can't be happening. She can't be here along with me and looking like this. I was about to call out to her when I realized there was one more person in the room. My dad. His old mustache was back. He looked young too.

I felt myself losing breath. I have entered some other dimension after the accident. That's what happened. It was too real to be a dream. I am sure about it. I did not know what to do when I heard him talk.

'Maya, we have been friends first and spouses later.' He

was close to whispering and I strained my ears to hear what they spoke.

'I am sorry but...I cannot let this happen.' He said. My mom started weeping.

'I don't know what to say...' She said to him softly.

'This is life Maya. You will have to put aside your feelings and forget everything for Nick. It's for his own good.' My dad was stern yet soft.

I saw my mother nodding at that. 'Yes, you might be right. Its not just us now....'

'And this idea of divorcing when Nick finishes his schooling...I don't think that will work either Maya. Our children are our responsibility and we have a life long commitment to them...we bought them to this world... it will hurt him if he came to know his mother and father divorced and his mother got married to another guy!' My dad continued. My mother started crying badly at this.

He left the kitchen and I ducked behind the couch in the living room. I saw him walk towards his bedroom and disappear. Once I made sure that he was out of sight, I tried coming out of my hiding place but stopped when I saw my mother come out of the kitchen towards the couch. She came and sat near our home LAN phone. She hesitated a bit before making a call. There was a long wait before someone answered on the other side.

'Yes, we talked.'

She hesitated again and started weeping again.

'Its not easy. Easy for you to say but not easy for us.' She was saying this to the person on the phone.

'My Nick will be affected and my husband is right in saying that. I am not sure this will work out...maybe ....we have to forget everything.'

That line got my attention and also my breath.

'You won't understand this Mathew! Why? Because you don't have a child.'

She disconnected the phone and sat there weeping for sometime. It was a heartbroken person that sat there. In between, she raised her head and looked straight ahead -the look of pain still on her face.

The streetlight outside had produced a slight glow inside the room. From between the couch and the side table I peered at her in that light.

Suddenly the look of pain was gone from her face and it turned into a menacing look. There was this oddly familiar smile on her face. Her gaze turned from the wall straight towards me. A horror took over me. For some reason I knew that this was not my mom. She got up and started towards where I was hiding. I moved away and crawled to the other end of the couch.

I know you are there Nikhil. She cooed.

There is no use hiding from me. I know you are there

I could hear her in my head again.

I sat there not uttering a word, my heart racing.

Come out my son. Don't you want to ask me something? What are you scared of?

I did not utter a word. I am not even sure if I felt anything anymore.

It better you come out and I promise you, you won't regret it.

I then forced myself to get up to look at her. She stood there in all her glory, in her nightdress, her hair open with that smile on her face and that look on her eyes...the same look I saw in my nightmare. I found my lips shivering as I tried to get my tongue to utter some words.

'Who are you?' *I asked her*

Oh my now what a question is that. You don't recognize your mother?

'What do you want?'

At this she started laughing.

You are smarter than I thought.

'What's happening?' I trembled as I asked her.

'Oh, you don't know the whole story, do you? Your mother was madly in love with your stepdad way before she met your dad. Your stepdad too loved her back with the same passion however, your grandparents were dead against him and took your mom away and ensured she never contacted your step dad! She even tried to kill herself but your grandfather who was an asshole was more stubborn than her and made plans to thus get your mother married at the earliest.'

My mother who was not my mother smiled before continuing.

'She couldn't talk to your dad before the wedding but just after the wedding, she informed him about the dilemma she was in. Your father who is too kind hearted and a stupid according to me was already in love with your mother and convinced her that if your stepdad really loved you, he would have contacted her by now.'

'Thus began a loveless marriage but a marriage where they both became very good friends. In the process, they had a child which was YOU. It was a one-off thing which bore fruit because you had to be born, hadn't you?'

She laughed at this. She moved closer to me and I could feel my whole body freezing up in fright.

'That's when your stepdad got in touch with her.' She said

coyly.

'He was chained down by his mother at first who threated to kill herself if he went pursuing your mother and later when he asked her to go to hell and came looking for your mother, met with an accident that put him in a wheelchair for over a year. Once out of it, his spirit was beaten, also his mother died. He then came to know that your mother got married and that broke his poor little heart' She chuckled at this.

'But fate, he came to Dubai too and he happened to meet your mom. Both of them realized they still love each other thus your mom went back to your dad and asked him if she could end the marriage? But your dad...he agreed on one condition that she wait till you finish your schooling.'

I couldn't believe any of this. I felt anger and sadness fill up in my heart along with the fright I felt.

'Now you had a problem with that arrangement also so I thought of changing things a little here, ok? And that's what happened now. There is no arrangement. Your father has straightly said that he wont allow this because you could be affected and that's what you saw happening there in that kitchen.' She had a crazy look on her face as she said that.

Suddenly she stopped talking and looked at me eerily.

'Aren't you happy with that too Nick?' The way she called me Nick sent shivers down my spine.

'I am...fine...' I muttered.

Good. Now whatever happens from here, hope that keeps you happy!

The air in the room suddenly felt still. The digital clock on the side table stood still too. It stood eerily at 2:22. The air felt heavier like in my nightmare.

Who ....are you...? I heard myself ask that in my head.

She walked towards me. I was frozen and couldn't move.

She touched my forehead with her right hand and before I knew I found myself falling into a dark hole screaming.

3

I woke up again in my old bed. I was sweating. The curtains were different this time though. The Donald duck was still on the side table but the picture in the frame was that of a 14 year old me. I sat up and looked around me. This time I did not hesitate and got up from the bed and slowly opened the door.

It was evening time. I realized that. The old familiarity greeted me again. I looked around in the corridor before heading to the kitchen again. This time there was no one there. I then heard noises–two people were arguing.

I edged closer to my parents room from where the noise was coming. The door was ajar and now the voices were clear.

They were arguing about something to do with a party. I could hear my mother trying to talk and my father not giving a chance. It was quite obvious that neither of them were listening to the other. They were full of rage and just trying to prove their point of view. I don't remember them being like this. They were always very happy with each other that when I came to know about their separation, I was shaken to the core which later resulted in my bitterness. I listened intently to understand what they were fighting about.

'You know very well that I never wanted to be with you!' Screamed my mother.

'Oh yes, you wanted to be with that no good S** of a ...' He stopped himself but I could hear him mumbling.

'Even he is not there in my life anymore, all because of you!' She screamed, 'And now you want me to act like the perfect wife in front of your colleagues! I can't do it!'

I heard a slap then and it was perfect stillness. That's when

I realized that I was holding my breath. I have never heard my parents fighting. Never. They have been the most pleasant couple you could ever meet .

I heard soft weeping from inside the room – it was my mother. I wanted to go inside and confront my dad.

'I am here. You can talk to me.' A voice behind me said. It sent a chill down my spine. I turned back to see my dad standing beside me. I did not see him come out. He looked exactly the way he was when I was a teenager. He had a smug look on his face.

Then I realized who stood there besides me. The fear was back again -its cold icy finger on my heart. All this while I knew that even though I met this thing, it never hurt me but for some reason I felt like I was near a lion which might leap at me anytime from under the bushes. I could feel my lower jaw numbing up.

'In case you are thinking of what is happening? This is the after effect of your dad wanting your mom to stay back. They are not happy with each other anymore! But I guess you are ok with this aren't you?'

I was about to open my mouth to tell him something but I couldn't talk. I wanted to ask him who is he and wanted to ask him to stop this

'You wanted this. Too late to stop anything now. Things are unfolding now. Enjoy.' He smirked at me and gave me a push.

It went dark. I was back in the damn bed again.

4

This time I got up from the bed immediately without even thinking twice or allowing myself to breathe in the air around me. I just wanted to know what is behind the door today. What shock or surprise awaits me. At the same time, a tentative fear gripped me. The fear of seeing that face in its different form. It obscured every loving image I had of my family members whosoever image it took. A wave of nausea washed over me. It was sudden and unexpected. That's when I wondered where the hell am I trapped? Is this all just a dream or is it something else? Everything felt so real. I could feel all the emotions. I could feel the things around me vividly. It couldn't be a dream. No. I never had dreams like this. I slowly opened the door and walked towards the kitchen. It was empty again. The clock on the wall showed it was afternoon.

There was Bob Marley silently crooning 'Three little birds' in the background. It was my mother's favorite song.

The dining table wasn't cleared–someone had left an untouched meal on it. I checked the contents. It was my mother's cup – I recognized it. Her favorite coffee mug which I had gifted her for mother's day. It had a picture of us with her at a coffee place. She loved that mug and used it for a very long time – as far I remember she was still using it even when I left home. The coffee was untouched now and cold. A plate of cold omelet made with mushrooms and chilli was on the table. My mother's favorite breakfast. Looks like she left it there in a hurry and went somewhere.

My father was no where to be seen. The date on the calendar made me understand my age to be 16.

I wanted to call out for my mom but decided then to keep quite and explore first. I did not expect my mom to come running for me – it would be someone or something else.

Something else.... It kept reverberating in my brain for no reason.

I tiptoed to my parents' room. Everything was in its place – in order and cleaned up just the way my mother would want it. Something lay on the bed. It was one of her valued possessions – a gold ring gifted to her by her father, my grandfather. I took the same in my hand. She had lost this when I was in my 11th grade and I remember her being very disappointed about the same. To see it thrown away very carelessly on the bed was very unlike her. My eyes fell on a small bag placed below the bed. A packed bag. I don't remember this bag very well but I was sure that this was a packed bag for someone ready to leave the house. My heart felt a bit faint. Is my mother planning to elope? I think I heard a faint far away laughter – that same sinister laughter and turned around to just a wisp of cold air. It sent a shiver through me.

I heard something like a movement coming from the bathroom and realized that my mother was in there. It hit me then that maybe she is indeed planning to elope with this person she was in love with for such a long time! I am sure I can convince her that this is wrong. I went towards the bathroom and saw that it was ajar. I took a long breath before opening the door.... Wishing with all my heart that it was indeed my mother ....

My thoughts dropped short as I felt myself slowly hyperventilating. Everything was vividly clear in front of my eyes. The bath tub, the curtains drawn to the side, the crimson red water and my mother half immersed in that water with her bloodied hands to the side, her eyes opened wide and facing up as if seeking for mercy. She had cut her wrists and I knew she was dead; it was there written all over her. There was blood everywhere.

I fell back unable to cry, looking at her. I couldn't take my eyes off her and her eyes. I couldn't breathe and I willed myself to get up , walking backwards and falling over a pile of clothes into the bedroom. My head hit the ground and I could feel tears coming up . I felt scared as I scrambled to my feet and ran to again hit and fall over a chair. That's when I started howling out loud.

I wanted to run from there and escape. I wanted to see it –

that thing. I wanted to ask why this was happening. I wanted to ask it to stop all this. But nothing happened.

That's when I realized that maybe this is my new reality.

I scrambled like a mad person back to my room . I could still hear bob marley singing 'Every little thing is going to be all right ...' in the background.

My dad sat on my bed.

The dull afternoon light lit up the room and he sat there with a glazed look in his eyes. I am not sure if he realized I was standing there at the doorway staring at him, my eyes filled with horror and pain.

His downcast eyes slowly found its way to me. He looked very old like the weight of the entire world rested on his shoulders.

A min passed with his stare on me, more like looking through me.

'Papa?' My sound creaked slowly. 'Ma.. is..'

'I know. I saw her. Its all my fault.' He said, calm and composed. He was not ok. It was very clear the way he was too calm.

'I did this to her. I tied her down. I came in between them. She had tried telling me ... that she can't do this . But I just acted like I understood her feelings and deep inside I thought that in due course of time all this will change ... But no....it didn't.'

I did not even know if he was speaking to me or someone else in the room, his eyes looked so lost.

'When you were born, I thought she would forget him... I never expected her to ... still be in love with him....'

'Why did she kill herself?' I shouted at him, tears running down my eyes.

'That guy Mathew, he killed himself. He was in depression

for a long time it seems. '

His voice trailed off. I felt goose bumps on my hands and feet.

He went silent again. I called out to him but he did not respond. He sat there frozen with that glazed look on his face. I went and hugged him and sat with him unable to move, unable to think.

'Don't cry. We can't do anything. I have called the police.' he said so emotionless that I looked at him. I wanted to shake him from his reverie.

A sort of numbness took over me. I was trapped here. This is the maybe that is now dished out to me. My mother is dead and my father seems catatonic. A tear found its way out of my eyes and before I knew it, I started wailing like a child. I just wanted to be out of here to what and where I was before the accident. I wanted to see 'Him' again and wanted to beg him to undo everything.

A night before I had everyone around me and now I sat lonely and wept. Maybe the what-ifs we always wish for may not be the best choice that life has to offer us.

Someone knocked at the door. At first I thought it must be my feeling. The knock continued persistent and I looked at my father who was still in a catatonic state. I slowly walked towards the door half frightened, half delirious. I opened the door to see the police and paramedics, neighbors and the likes....

They were asking me many questions. I did not hear anything.

'Where is your dad?' Someone pulled me towards him to ask and I fought them to leave me alone.

They said I should be sedated because I was screaming like a mad person. I wasn't screaming. I was just asking people to leave me alone. I had not called anyone, not even the police.

Where did they come from? Then I remembered what my dad told me. He had called them.

Someone put a soothing hand over my shoulder and asked me to calm down. She had a loving look on her face and reminded me of my mom. I cried again uncontrollably.

I heard someone asking for my dad .I heard a commotion in my bedroom. I pushed everyone aside to go to my room. Suddenly it felt like there were so many people in my room.

I saw two men trying to restrain my dad as he tried to fight them. He was going crazy just like me. I rushed towards them and started hitting the men, trying to free my dad.

I could hear myself screaming as someone pulled me back and I felt something cold pierce my hand. My scream grew fainter as everything around me swam towards nothingness and my heart beat started slowing down. I felt myself being placed somewhere soft.

'You need rest', I heard a soft voice. The digital clock on the table was edging towards 2:22

'I love....my mom...I ...' It went dark

Bob Marley played on the background still.

5

I opened my eyes in a hospital bed. It was dark and silent around me. Someone opened the door in front of me and walked inside and all I could hear were the beep of the machines. I couldn't get up from my bed even as I tried. A terror filled my heart.

Even before he appeared in front me, I could smell the fear of him deep down my gut. Maybe now he will do something to me?

'What do you want?', I whispered

He stood in the shadows and chuckled.

'It wasn't me. It was YOU who wanted ...things to be different.'

'I didn't want my family to be destroyed.' I said feeling weak.

He chuckled again

'You asked for it Nick.' The sarcasm very evident in the voice. I was being mocked, played with and made to suffer.

'You love your mother and yet you wanted to see her suffer... you don't like seeing your dad or your mother happy. In fact you can't stand it. And your little brother...tch..tch... like a bully you broke his little angels ...you big bad boy, you!' He laughed hard at this.

I did not utter a word at this. I could feel tears stinging my eyes.

'Please.... Please undo this. I want my mother back. I .... I want my dad back...'

'Oh, don't cry. I told you. You are better off being that asshole you were. I had great expectations of you but you disappoint me.' He sounded bored.

'Please...' I begged him, 'I would rather see them alive and happy than lose them.' I cried.

He laughed at this.

'Are you.... are you the devil himself...?' I croaked

'You humans.... You think you know everything...' He said sarcastically. He walked towards me.

Closer.

I held my breath and closed my eyes. I could feel his

breath on me.

'How you disappoint me Nick!' He said in a dramatic tone.

A slimy finger fell on me and I screamed. I was in the dark again.

I felt someone pushing me back to where I was lying. I couldn't breathe and wondered if something was dragging my soul down into the depths of hell. I realized that I couldn't open my eyes. It was me melting away in heat and confusion and terror while trying to gasp for air. It was me fighting for some sort of survival. When the voices reached me, I did not understand anything what it said.

'Calm down....'

I thought I heard it wrong

'Breathe...', I heard a faint noise.

I stopped struggling then and forced myself to breathe.

I heard a familiar voice now – my mothers.

'Nick, it's me. I am here beside you.' She has come to take me...At last. A sort of calm took over me then. This is what they say about peaceful death.

I was able to breathe again; the pressure on my body was off. I opened my eyes to very bright light and people around me. My mother was one of them.

'Oh Nick.' She wept, 'You are back. We thought we lost you!!'

There was a doctor and 2 nurses with her. The doctor looked at me with calm eyes and understood what I wanted to ask him.

'You were in an accident Nick and unconscious for the last 24 hours.' He said with grave concern in his eyes.

6

I had slammed my car into the four-wheeler and gone into a temporary coma. They found me unconscious and bleeding like a broken pipe inside my car. I was rushed to the hospital and I had survived miraculously without much damage to my body other than a broken leg and hand.

My father and mother stayed besides me all the time until today when out of the blue my body started jerking violently. The doctors thought I was having the seizures until they realized that I was trying to get up from the bed though I was still unconscious. They held me down and asked my mother to call out to me, which was when I calmed down. They were however very surprised when I opened my eyes then and there itself.

The preceding days after that I was still very cautious. I was not ready to believe that I was in the real world. Maybe this is again one of his plays to test me. His make-believe world where suddenly one of them might turn up to me and start chuckling. *'You believed it's all over, didn't you! Well it's not!'*

My constant silence concerned my family. My mother would try feeding me while I was in hospital and I would avoid her eyes. She once asked me softly why I found it difficult to look at her and the image of her lying with that look of horror on her face would pop up in my mind and I would start crying.

She hugged me tight and cried with me.

'Shhh...it's alright.' She assured me.

I did not see my dad until a day after I woke up. He stood at the doorway looking at me. It was not the dead eyes I saw him last in. There was concern and pain in them. He came and hugged me though we exchanged no words. I knew he wanted to say that he was happy to see me back.

Within days I was back home and my mom decided to

stay with me for sometime to nurse me back to health.

Days passed and I slowly regained my strength though mentally I was still fighting to be normal again. I avoided looking at the clock or checking the time on the phone. I was scared of seeing those numbers again 2:22. I would only check when I was sure I won't be seeing those numbers.

I never discussed my experience with anyone for fear of being mocked or dismissed as hallucinations of a guy who survived a major accident. Maybe I did hallucinate all of it – I can't be sure, can I? But I know that it was too vivid to be dismissed as one. There are nights after I have lain awake too afraid to sleep in the fear of going back there – the land of maybes. My maybe did not turn out to be too good.

I joined back my dads firm soon after. I apologized to Arun and became good friends with him. I slowly built my relation with my step dad and my step mom and also with Nathan. A few months later on my birthday, when he gifted me a hand made card that said 'To the world's best brother' I had tears in my eyes. I then wondered what had got over my head all that time when I buried myself in self pity and loathing and chose to ignore all the positivity around me.

A year passed and it was Christmas time again. This time it was different. I was a happy man. My parents and my step-parents loved me. I got beautiful new angels for Nathan. He was so happy that he yelped with joy and hugged me tight. That night after the Christmas dinner, I was out in the balcony taking a smoke when my dad joined me.

The night air was cold but we enjoyed it. My dad looked at me and said

'Nick, I know that all is good now. I just want you to know that I did what I did because I felt it was the right thing.'

I nodded at him.

'I know everything dad. I know everything.' I looked into

his eyes.

'Maybe had I not done it...' He started.

'Don't even think of the maybe dad. This is the best *maybe* you have taken.' I told him smiling. He smiled back at me, his eyes twinkling with joy.

I smiled as I heard my mother call out to us from inside of the house

'Dessert is served guys. Come in!'

Acknowledgement

They say that gratitude is the best attitude. This page is a token of gratitude for all those people who helped put this book and the dream of mine into a reality.

I thank Almighty and the Universe for all the incidents that pushed me towards writing this book keeping my insecurities folded up in the cupboard. Sometimes things happen to open way to new experiences in life.

I thank my husband for backing me up on my dream and for being a hardcore critique of my work.

I also thank my mom and my sister-in-law for taking time to read the stories and in being genuine in their feedbacks.

I thank the entire team of Invincible publishers – without you guys, this dream was only half possible. It was always very easy to talk and deal with you all.

Last but not the least, thanks to you readers, whoever decided to pick up this book to give me a chance to entertain your day.

Thank you all so much.

About the Author

Nitya enjoys expressing herself through written words and loves reading and writing intriguing and dark stories. Born in India, she has spent most of her life in the sunny city of Dubai where she currently resides with her family with lots of sunshine and happiness around her. She is currently on a break from her corporate job.

When she is not reading or writing, she is busy chasing out the neighbor's cat, window-shopping or spending time with her kids. ***What the Eyes See*** is her debut book.